Check for Junk.

By

Don Allen

Dedication.

To My parents who raised me right.

ISBN: 979-8-9877821-3-2

eISBN: 979-8-9877821-2-5

Publisher: Don Allen

1: First Night

'It was a dark and stormy night' .... wait, that's the start of another story. Actually, it was the middle of the night, a humid Floridian night, with a new moon and a cloudless sky as I drove the van into the warehouse. As the overhead door was being pulled down, two of Tony's men walked up to the van, opened the sliding door, and unceremoniously pulled Jeromy out.

Jeromy is my partner. Together, we provided discrete investigative services. The name of our endeavor is *El Ojo Privado*, Spanish for *The Private Eye*, not creative but catchy. We have been in business together for about three years. Jeromy is a washed-up, second-tier boxer; he provides the muscle. Me, I'm George Basdakis, a college graduate with a BA in history; thank you. And thanks to the Navy's ROTC program, I served six years in the Navy, departing with the rank of Lieutenant.

Tony had hired us to locate stolen cash. Apparently, one hundred thousand was missing from his office. We will get into where it came from in a bit, but for now, the task was to find the money. He gave us two leads. One was a corrupt cop, Detective

Nathan Wrisley, who sprung a warrantless search of Tony's premises last month. The money was found to be missing shortly after the search. Complicating the case, one of Tony's men disappeared soon after the cash was found missing.

The easy part was finding the missing man. We tracked him to Tennessee. His mother had been admitted to a hospice care facility. He wanted to be with her during her last days. He had no money.

That left the corrupt cop. This was a bit more problematic given he could set us up on a contrived offense, so we burgled his house. Under the floorboards in his bedroom, we found the cash; ten packets of one-hundred, hundred-dollar bills.

We turned the money over to Tony, collected a handsome fee, and went our separate ways.

Did I mention Jeromy was a boxer? He was slow on the uptake after losing numerous knockout decisions. When we recovered the cash, one packet of bills made its way into his back pocket. He didn't realize, and to be fair, I didn't either, that all the bills had sequential serial numbers. A week later he attracted Tony's attention when using one-hundred-dollar bills like confetti at *Bennie's*, a local bar with questionable women.

Tony, or more aptly his two enforcers, 'suggested' I bring Jeromy to the warehouse that night -- or I'd go down with him. So here we were in Tony's warehouse, Jeromy tied to a chair, and Tony told me I was free to go.

Now many will ask about loyalty to one's teammate. Over the past three years, Jeromy screwed me on several deals, short-changed me in cash transactions, and forgot to post bail for one of my more embarrassing incidents. Jeromy's level of compassion rivaled that of a scorpion, but he was good with clients. For some strange reason, he had a calming effect on them. Jeromy was a useful business partner when it fit his needs.

2: George Basdakis

As I said, I'm George. I was born on the 23rd of April 1976, *Agios Georgios Day*, better known as St. George's Day. I grew up on the Gulf Coast. My father and his older brother, Greek immigrants, owned a small fishing fleet in Biloxi, Mississippi. I'm the youngest of five boys, ten years younger than the next in line. My mother called me 'her surprise.' She taught me Greek, and to my brothers' dismay, she and I would have conversations they couldn't understand.

Growing up my best buddy was my cousin, Nicholas. He is the son of my father's younger brother, Christos. We're about the same age, and many took us for twins. Before Christos moved his business to Mobile, we attended the same Greek Orthodox elementary school and drove the nuns to distraction. On more than one occasion we were subject to the same corporal punishment since the offended party couldn't differentiate between the two of us, and the principal knew we both were guilty of something. My knowledge of Greek often curbed their discussions of the 'twins' as they referred to us.

When I was young I'd ask my parents where we came from. Where were my grandparents? They were evasive, saying we came from Greece, but it was a messy story; they'd tell me someday when I was older.

4

***

One summer, I was twelve, maybe thirteen years old was spent with Nicholas in Mobile. I'm not sure whose idea it was, but we decided to shoplift some new footwear. A new line of sneakers had just come out, endorsed by some long-forgotten sports star and selling for an exorbitant price.

We had an elaborate plan. We'd go into the mall shoe store, try on the sneakers, and tie the laces together when re-boxing them. A few moments later, ten minutes or less, Nicholas sets off a string of Chinese firecrackers in a trash can in the mall's concourse. With the distraction, I grabbed the sneakers from their boxes. Running out of the store, I tossed Nicholas his, and with sneakers hanging around our necks, we headed for our bikes in the parking lot.

It's only fair to note here 'our' bikes were from a local playground in the adjacent, more affluent neighborhood. The Mall Cops were out in force, we had to detour into the depths of the parking lot. As the cops swarmed the area, Nicholas and I hid under a pickup truck. As the hue 'n cry moved down the rows of cars, we made a break for the woods bordering the south side of the complex. We were seen. "There they are!!" yelled one of the cops. We tore through the woods like animals chased by rabid coon hounds, crossed a small creek, and waded through the edge of a swamp hoping the gators were asleep. We evaded capture. Along the way, we lost 'our' new sneakers.

5

Christos looked at us as we came into the house. "You look like you've been dragged through the swamp," he says. Not far from the truth, I'm thinking.

***

In high school, we drifted apart. I was a jock; Nicholas was a delinquent. After one unfortunate incident, he accidentally shot a buddy; the Judge suggested that Nicholas join the army as an alternative to the juvenile detention center. I went to college; Nicholas was off to Fort Polk.

Today I'm a six-foot adorable hulk, or so women say. Many older ladies claim I have Paul Neman's sparkling blue eyes. I maintain the two hundred pounds I had in college and still display six-pack abs; why? I have no idea since I never work out.

While my brothers worked on the fishing boats, my mother kept me home. My father acquiesced to her demands. Despite being a mama's boy, I excelled in high school sports and managed to land a football scholarship to the University of Mississippi.

Despite my best efforts, if one discounted partying, I remained on the second-string team for two years. The coach put me in in my junior season after the backup quarterback was injured. This was my chance to shine. But, I had a bet riding on the game, a large bet that Ole Miss would lose.

I knew my bookie was betting on the spread. We were perilously close to narrowing the point spread. In the fourth quarter, I had my chance. The play called for the quarterback to run the ball. Linemen opened a hole for me, and I was off. Twenty yards to the goal line. Ten and no opposition in sight; I tripped! The ball was recovered by the Aggies. I blamed a divot in the field.

Later Coach Rowland strongly suggested I drop off the team. "George, I'd take disciplinary action against you if I had any proof you were gambling on that game. Don't give me the crap you tripped. If I see you in the locker room again, I'll pay the team to beat you to a pulp."

Now, I may be many things, but stupid is not one of them. I took the coach's advice.

To the chagrin of my father, I majored in history. My father's first question was always, "Where do you plan to get a job?" My brothers were not far behind with their taunts. My mother was my sole supporter. She died late in my junior year.

Early on at Ole Miss, I joined the Navy ROTC program, and it wasn't for the small stipend ROTC provided, but it did help in my decision-making. My father stopped all financial support by my senior year. The stipend helped, but it was the money I received from my bookie that got me through my last year at Ole Miss. I graduated in the middle of the pack, but unlike most classmates, I had no student debt.

3: My Navy Career

I was commissioned as a Navy Ensign in 1998. My first duty station was San Diego, where I prepped for sea duty on a destroyer for the next six months. In my off hours, I became intimately familiar with Tijuana. I could usually be found at *el Perro Salado*, known better as *The Salty Dog* to us gringos. It was off the beaten track and hosted questionable characters. Its main attraction was Felina, who would whirl to the music.

One Saturday, I got it into my head to flirt with Felina. She was more than receptive. As she whirled by, she landed in my lap. After a bit of giggling, she whirled around the room. A bit later, a large dude, a jarhead, probably stationed at Camp Pendleton, sat himself at my table, uninvited, and handed me a bottle of beer. His first words were, "Keep your hands off her, she's mine." He then indicated a table where two of his buddies were sitting. "You won't make it back across the border if you look at her again." He then gets up with a big smile and struts back to his buddies.

Louis, one of The Salty Dog's regulars, asks, "What was that about? I can solve that problem for you amigo."

"No, let it go, just a blowhard."

As Louis and his friends leave the bar, one of the seedier ones plants a ten-inch bowie knife into the jarhead's table. The three of them, a bit shaken, are staring at the still-quivering blade when I unceremoniously plunk myself down at the table.

"Friend, a word of advice, don't threaten strangers; sometimes they bite. Felina is not worth your life." I leave, and my bottle of beer is sitting on their table. I never saw them again.

On occasion, I could be found consorting with Louis. I was his some-time money mule, moving funds from his dealer in San Diego to Tijuana. Now where the money came from, I didn't want to know, and where it was going, I didn't ask, other than the small portion I received.

It was a simple operation. Friday evening I'd stop at Gilley's Tavern in National City, order a Pacifico beer, the barkeep would slip me an envelope filled with cash, usually eight or nine thousand dollars in one-hundred-dollar bills, and I'd stuff it in my pants. The next stop was the border crossing at San Ysidro. I had a preferred parking lot just north of the pedestrian crossing point. From there it was a twenty-minute walk to *The Salty Dog*. Why did I do this? The risk was negligible, and payments from Louis helped extend my meager Ensign's paycheck.

***

Late in my stay in San Diego, I got a call from my father's lawyer, Mr. Johnson. I can only remember meeting him once when the court threatened to take title to my father's boats over some legal issue I didn't understand. He was calling to tell me my father and Uncle Mecho were dead; the fishing boat exploded in the harbor. All aboard were killed. An inquest was being held in ten days. The court wanted to know if I planned on attending.

"What happened?" I asked.

"We don't know; it's now a homicide investigation."

After I disconnected from Mr. Johnson, I called Christos, my father's youngest brother, in Mobile.

"Uncle Christos, dad's lawyer just called telling me he and Mecho were dead, their fishing boat blown up. What's going on?"

"They were targeted by enemies from the old country," said Christos. "I don't think your parents ever told you about the family's past. I never told Nicolas."

Before we left Greece in the '60s, your father, Mecho, your mother, and I were in the underground fighting Georgios Papadopoulos's dictatorship. Your father made some serious enemies when he and Mecho firebombed the homes of some minor officials. Their families promised retribution. Two of the sons managed to locate us last year. They set off the bombs with remote detonators. They are now in police custody."

"I'll be there late tomorrow," I said.

"No! You stay where you are. There may be others seeking revenge on the family. You and I are the only family members here; Nicolas is on his second tour in Iraq. And I have no idea where my oldest brother is; still in Greece I think."

"There are no bodies and only a memorial service to be held by the Greek Fisherman Association. You weren't that close to your father or uncle, so stay where you are and be safe."

***

We finally got orders to join the 7th Fleet in Hawaii. The evening before we were to weigh anchor, I visited Gilley's Tavern for one last time. As expected, he had an envelope for Louis. Later, back on the ship, I counted $7,300 that Louis would not be receiving. I won't be visiting The Salty Dog anytime soon!

4: Fat Leonard

As the junior officer on the USS Ford, I got all the shit details. I was a Lieutenant, Junior Grade, by the time the ship was reassigned to the 7th Fleet. We made many port calls, most in Singapore, for both shore leave and to be resupplied. One of my favorite haunts was *Bugis Street.*

In the daytime Bugis Street was a typical shopping area. Some high-end stores but mostly small mom & pop enterprises. But after midnight the street was barricaded, curbside tables set up, and a horde of vendors with their pushcarts descended, and *Bogie Street* awakened.

The delicacies served by the street vendors rivaled those of the city's five-star chefs. Some vendors served Chinese, others Indian curry; curry so hot it'd singed one's nose hairs just smelling it. Malaysian delicacies and Indonesian treats were featured by other vendors. Young boys served as waiters, weaving in and out between the tables. It is rumored one could arrange to buy almost anything here. Let one of the boys know what you're looking for, and before you ordered your next beer, a dealer would show up; RPGs, small arms, stolen art -- all available.

Tourists flocked to the area. The British in their kaki 'bush' attire. The Germans somberly dressed; the French more formally attired. The Japanese tour groups nestled around tour guides with their little flags. But Americans stood out, dressed in Hawaiian garb, just off a Disney cruise ship.

On one corner, a blind Chinese beggar played an old Chinese one-string fiddle, a tambura, I think it's called. The catgut string sounded as if the cat was being channeled back to the living.

It is here that I first met 'Fat Leonard.' He was a big man, a 350-pound, 6-foot Malaysian businessman. It was early morning, let's say 1:30 a.m. I was sitting at a curbside table sipping Tiger Balm Beer, one of the best beers in Asia, when a large gent approached and asked, "Do you mind if I sit here." Looking up at him, I invited him to join me.

He was very congenial, and we soon got into a philosophical discussion.

"See all those attractive young ladies," he asked. There were several sitting not far from us. "Most work as nightclub hostesses. They congregate here after the city's curfew calls for the closure of clubs at midnight. They're all transvestites."

"No way! That one in the blue is as feminine as any woman I've ever seen!"

Leonard smiles and calls a boy over. "Ask the lady in the blue to join us," pointing to her while slipping a bill to him.

He does, and soon she is sauntering over to our table and with a smile, asks, "What can I do for you?"

"Have a seat," Leonard says, pushing out the chair next to me.

She sits, he continues, "My friend here thinks you are a woman; let him have a feel."

She bristles, "What do you think I am, a piece of meat for sale?" she snarls, getting up.

"Yes," laying a hundred-dollar Singapore banknote on the table.

She picks up the bill and sits back down.

"Okay, George, run your hand down there and tell me what you find."

I look at him, look at her, and cautiously slip my hand up under her dress. As I find 'his' junk, 'she' smiles saying, "George, my room is not far from here. Shall we go?"

As I recoil, my fingers feel as if they've been burnt. Leonard is laughing, and our young friend asks if there is anything else 'she' can do before returning to her friends."

He was the owner of Leonard's Chandler Services. On a subsequent outing with Fat Leonard, he tells me his main business is providing dockside services. He *can* provide ship services, resupply, minor maintenance, etc., for prices far cheaper than other ship chandlers. There could be a finder's fee. We hit it off.

At the time I was the USS Ford's assistant maintenance officer. Lieutenant Commander Fugate, the maintenance officer, had been hospitalized at the Naval Hospital on Guam for an ailment he contracted on shore leave in Hawaii. I introduced the ship's Captain, Commander Chapin, to Fat Leonard at one of the parties Leonard hosted. I didn't know the Commander could drink that much and never suspected his roving eye for the ladies. Over the next year, the USS Ford made frequent use of Leonard's Chandler Services. By the end of the year, I had a nice bank balance in a numbered account in Indonesia that Leonard helped me set up.

Late in 2002, the Navy Criminal Investigative Service, NCIS, took an active interest in Fat Leonard. The USS Ford was attracting particular scrutiny due to its frequent use of Leonard's Chandler Services. As the investigation ramped up, Commander Chapin was relieved of command for possible fraud.

I was promoted to Lieutenant in February of 2003, possibly because of my behind-the-scenes cooperation with NCIS that led to the arrest of Fat Leonard -- and several senior Naval officers.

***

The USS Ford was redeployed to the Persian Gulf that February as part of the naval buildup for the Iraqi War. It was an uneventful deployment, mostly dodging Iranian-armed speedboats that swarmed US warships. One night when I had the bridge, a swarm of a dozen speedboats circled the three American naval vessels: the USS Ford, her sister destroyer, and a supply ship.

We were anchored twenty miles from Failaka Island, putting us in Kuwaiti waters. I thought they were overly aggressive and ordered the bow gunner to open fire with the deck-mounted .50 caliber machine gun. This action caused the other destroyer to join the fray. In short order, the supply ship's forward 20 mm cannon was active. In less than a few minutes, three of the speedboats were going under. The remaining boats fled. I ordered the deck crew to launch a boat to recover survivors. The next morning the Fleet's Vice Admiral had me flown to US Naval Headquarters at the Bahrain Naval Base.

Thinking my goose was cooked, I put my best face on and reported to the board of inquiry. After being ripped for causing the US international embarrassment, the Vice Admiral in charge of the board pulled me aside during a break, "Lieutenant, I want to congratulate you on the action you took. If the woke weenies in our State Department had your testicular fortitude, we could have this mess cleaned up in six months. But that's not the world we live in. Before this hearing goes any further, I recommend you resign your commission and leave the field with honor."

So in 2004, after serving in the Navy for six years, I departed with the rank of Lieutenant. I was ready for a change. I had close to a quarter million dollars, American, in an Indonesian bank.

I flew to Jakarta, arriving late Friday night. This was my first visit to the city, and it was mostly unimpressive. So much so

16

Indonesia is moving its Capital from Jakarta to another island. Why? In addition to the congestion, Jakarta is sinking; annual flooding is getting worse. Now environmentalists will tell you it's climate change. But, does the fact that Jakarta is the world's fastest-sinking city matter? No, it's climate change they yell! The city has sunk two and a half meters over the past century. That's not good for a coastal city that, for the most part, sits inches above sea level.

When the bank opened the following Monday, I walked in upbeat, planning on withdrawing a sizable amount in cash and transferring the balance to my Navy Credit Union Account. I provided the teller with the account number and my password. After an initial delay, the teller kept punching keys on his keyboard; I was getting worried. I became concerned when he left the window to consult with the manager. The manager called me into his office.

Mr. Murphy, there are only five thousand dollars in your account. Last year you transferred a quarter million to an unknown account. A sinking feeling told me Fat Leonard screwed me. He drained my account, leaving only enough for a ticket home. The bank manager checked my account information one more time, then, turning to his desk, retrieved an envelope addressed to me. In it was a single piece of paper. The message: *Always Check for Junk*, signed Leonard Francis.

5: Florida

Fat Lenard left me enough money for a business-class ticket to Miami and change left over for a taxi. It was a long flight with one plane change in Los Angles, giving me plenty of time to contemplate my future. My father's constant refrain, "Where do you plan to get a job" rang in my ears. I was a 30-year-old stud with a Bachelor of Arts in European History and wasn't even qualified to be a barista.

At the depth of feeling sorry for myself, a name emerged from my subconscious, Michael Zych. He was my drinking buddy at Ole Miss. What he lacked in scruples, he made up for in smarts. He graduated a year ahead of me and went on to law school. Through the school's grapevine, I heard he passed the Florida Bar Exam and was practicing in Miami. Why should he help me you may be asking? He made some significant coin betting on a certain football game. He owed me!

The taxi dropped me at a nondescript row of storefronts in downtown Miami. Michael's office was on the second floor, in a corner office, with an outer office for his secretary. The office's one redeeming feature was its location, a block and a half from the Dade County District Courthouse.

In the outer office, I found a young Latina, the nameplate on the desk identified her as Angelic Morales. "Is Mr. Zych in?" I asked.

"Do you have an appointment?"

"No, I'm here to collect on a bar bill from Ziggy's. Interest has pushed up the amount due to over a thousand dollars." She paled a bit given this was probably far more than the office's petty cash box had.

She pressed the buzzer and a moment later Michael appeared with a golf putter in his hand.

Tossing the putter aside, he grabs me, "George, what brings you to town? Come on in. Angelic, can you get us two cold beers please." Looking at me, "There's a convenience store downstairs," he says, anticipating any comment on my part.

We do a quick catch-up, me describing my role in the Fat Leonard scandal, the shooting gallery in the Persian Gulf, my hasty exit from the Navy, and my empty bank account in Jakarta.

As Michael walks me to the door, he says, "...wish there was something I could do for you, but..."

Pausing at the door, "I've given that some thought," I said. "You have a small practice here, defending questionable people, some with hidden secrets. I'm proposing you hire me as your private investigator. You never know what I can find; for instance, how you got the money to buy that new Corvette in your last year at school."

I have his attention. "What will this cost me?" he asks.

"A one-time retainer fee of twenty-five hundred, upfront, with all future fees linked to specific clients."

6: El Ojo Privado

Not long after associating myself with Michael, he tossed me a bone. "George, if you would, I need to talk to you. I have a case, a divorce case. The wife thinks the husband is hiding assets. I want you to find them. As an incentive, the wife is offering 10 percent of whatever you find; yours to keep."

Ursula Scott's scumbag of a husband netted me three hundred thousand dollars. He had three million hidden in an offshore account that I was able to track down by ... well let's not talk about unsavory details. The end result was Ursula got her divorce, with a big payday; Michael made a nice fee in addition to burnishing his reputation at the courthouse; and most importantly, my bank account had a large positive balance.

Over the past few months, taking online classes, I was able to pass the State of Florida's private investigator exam. I am now a card-carrying PI, just like Jim Rockford. My military background helped in getting a concealed carry permit, but I don't keep my .38 in a cookie jar.

Last month I opened my office, *El Ojo Privado*, a floor above Michael's. After our initial rough start, one could say I blackmailed him into our relationship, we've worked well together. I'm now his 'go-to guy' to find things, much like Paul Drake was for Perry Mason. I've successfully worked several cases for him.

He has sent me a few clients. I've even been able to refer a few to him, although the last two were hardcore and are now living in state facilities, and Michael is still waiting to get paid.

Most days we finish up at Helen's; I've grown to enjoy her mojitos. Helen is an elderly Greek matriarch, probably in her late 70s, with a large extended family in the Miami area. She's owned a bar in Miami for the past fifty years. The bar's motif, Helen of Troy of course. One wall has a painting of a Trojan Horse. The other walls depict Greek warriors storming the gates of Troy. Entering the bar the first thing one sees is a life-size painting of Paris with Helen over his shoulder. This Helen has the younger face of the bar owner.

When she learned I was Greek, named after St. George, I was adopted. Helen's family members, although not in high places, were entrenched in the city's businesses and municipal institutions. In the following months, they proved invaluable.

In one case a cuckold husband wanted dirt on his wife's lover. She was a law clerk at one of the city's more prestigious law firms, the lover, a partner. Gregory, one of Helen's grandsons, was able to provide me access to the building where the law firm was a tenet and I was able to get photos of the randy couple on the corporate balcony no less. Gregory received a generous tip and my fee netted a tidy sum.

Helen was not above a little manipulation. One evening after a mojito or three she slides up beside me at the bar, orders a bottle of Retsina, and pours me a glass. I waive it off. "A good Greek boy like you won't share some good Greek wine with your hostess?"

"White wine flavored with pine pitch is not my thing," I say. "Let me get us some Ouzo."

"Can't stand the stuff" she quips, "that's all my late husband drank. Disgusting stuff!"

"George, can you do an old lady a favor? I have a friend, an elderly widow with a problem. She is sitting in the booth over there. Would you talk with her?"

How could I say no?

I went to the widow's booth and sat across from her. She was frail and obviously traumatized. "Helen said you have a problem that I might be able to help you with."

She starts to tear up as she passes an envelope to me. I open it; the note inside demands a thousand dollars if she wants Fluffy back. It directs her to leave the money in the dog park under the 'green' stone. "I let Fluffy into the backyard to do her business first thing every morning," she says. "This morning she disappeared. I found this envelope with her collar on my doorstep. I can't pay this amount; can you help get my Fluffy back?"

Now with Helen watching from the bar, what can I do?

"Yes, tell me about the green stone." This would be a pro-bono case, the poor lady lived social security check to social security check.

A day later after researching other missing dogs in the neighborhood, there were several, I started to see a pattern emerge. One elderly gentleman reported paying five hundred dollars to get his bulldog back.

Now, who could snatch dogs and be invisible? Animal control came to mind. One of Helen's great-nieces worked at the county's animal shelter. At noontime, I found her on the job and asked a few questions. She pointed me to a new county hire, a new dog catcher, a strange guy, not very talkative. She gave me his schedule; I found him and followed him home. Guess what I found in his backyard? A toy poodle. Now, it could have been his but he didn't look like a poodle kind of guy. After some 'friendly' questioning he admitted to dognapping.

I returned Fluffy to the widow who was at a loss for words to express her thanks.

Our dognapper was fired, was tried in court for a misdemeanor, and put on probation. His neighbors weren't so forgiving. For them, justice was dog crap in the mailbox, dog crap dumped in his front yard, and dog crap in his car. He attempted to file a harassment complaint with the police ... the desk sergeant was a dog lover.

7: Monet

One bright morning Michael favors my office with a visit. "Still no secretary I see, who gets your coffee?"

"And good morning to you too, what brings you up to the third floor ... a better view of the courthouse?

"Actually I may have a client for us," Michael continues after our opening banter. "As you know, the County Courthouse has a small fitness center. Officers of the court are encouraged to join, for a not-so-nominal fee. Fees for judges and prosecutors are covered under their employment contracts. The rest of us poor shmucks are stuck with an annual, two-thousand-dollar membership fee. Now, I'm not complaining mind you, this is cheap for networking opportunities. By the way, your 8X10 of the two getting it on, on the Okan Tower terrace, is still posted on the fitness center's bulletin board."

"Now to the point, one of the junior prosecutors is looking for someone to represent his sister-in-law in her divorce proceedings. This is not going to be a simple divorce. It's going to be messy. She's an exotic dancer at one of the city's upscale nightclubs. Her husband is a popular radio personality. They've been married three months and acrimonious charges have been flying since the honeymoon. She is charging him with infidelity. This is where you come in, she wants proof!"

25

"Sounds like fun. When do I start?"

She will be in my office at two this afternoon. Stay by your phone. Angelic will call when we are ready for you."

Midafternoon Angelic calls me down to Michael's office. Entering his inner chamber I see a modern-day Venus. Her name is Monet, with an enchanting French accent. She's tall, slim, porcelain features, and raven black hair. It's my conclusion her husband is a jerk.

After an introduction, we get down to business, my fee. "One hundred fifty dollars an hour, plus expenses," I say.

Without blinking, she writes me a check for five thousand dollars, "Your retainer" she says.

Monet gives me the background on Jimmy, 'Jimmy the Freak' as he's known to his radio audience. She lists his hangout places; identifies various bed mates, and where I can find them. She sums it up with, "I want pictures!"

After she leaves, Michael and I compare notes. He advises me, "Keep it in your pants, former lovers call her *the viper*."

Where to start? I look at the information Monet provided. It's getting close to happy hour so I decide to visit the Freak's favorite watering hole, *Bennie's*. Bennie's is just inside 'Little Cuba.' The bar's name is a holdover from the '40s. Benny was a Gunny Sargent who died on Imo Jima. Legend has it he was the first Marine ashore. It's a tough crowd.

Jimmy is not there. A few discreet questions, wrapped in franklins, netted me Jennet, the name of his current flame, a name not on Monet's list. Jennet has a beach house up the road in Hollywood. It's early in the evening so I decide a drive-by might be in order. At 1313 South Surf Road I find a well-maintained bungalow, probably built in the early '60s. Its side, both sides, are encased by mature bougainvillea hedges. The back appears to be open to the beach.

One of the contacts I've developed over the past year is Federico. He's a computer genius and a drone devotee. If the price is right, he's a pillar of support. The price was right and that weekend we staked out a spot in the public park on the beach, just down the road from 1313 South Surf Rd.

Midafternoon Federico launches the drone. The drone carried a high-resolution camera with a decent telephoto lens. Flying about fifty to seventy-five yards offshore we flew up and down the beach panning yards facing the sea. After a couple of passes, and no evidence of occupancy at 1313 South Surf Road, we wrap it up for the day. I spend the rest of the weekend trying to locate Jimmy. He seems to have evaporated. He even had a guest host on his radio show. On vacation?

Our third weekend of drone surveillance netted results. Bingo, we have two bodies, next to the pool at our target house. The drone was on station for fifteen or twenty minutes when the two bodies merged.

"Federico, take it in for a closer look." At about ten yards off the shore, it was obvious Jimmy and Jennet were violating Jimmy's marital oath. Federico was mesmerized, the drone drifts closer to the target. Jimmy's head pops around as he hears the buzz from the propellers. Excellent, a great facial shot of both of them as she lays under him looking up.

"Get the bird back here, we need to leave before he starts looking for us." As my nondescript car merged into traffic, Jimmy's red BMW was swinging into the park's parking lot.

Monday morning I share my photos with Michael. "I think we can update the one in the gym's locker room," he sniggers. "Jimmy the Freak's goose is cooked!"

By the end of the week, Jimmy agrees to a no-contest divorce, and to cover Monet's expenses … which includes my fee.

Monet invited both Michael and me to the club where she was performing. I don't get embarrassed often, but when she invites me onto the stage, I was blushing as she dances around the stage wearing … I'm not sure what it was but it didn't cover munch.

Later in her dressing room, she thanks us both, giving Michael a check for ten thousand dollars as a bonus. She tells me to keep the balance of my retainer and hands me a bonus check for five thousand. Easiest money I ever made – or so I thought.

8: Expansion

A few months later Monet still frequents my dreams. Jimmy, not so much.

When one of my new clients, Rosco, wants to visit Benny's I didn't give it a second thought. My client, an elderly retiree from New York, a retired Marine, wants to visit the bar.

"George, you ever hear of Benny's Bar? My father was in his platoon and saw Benny go down. He was hit seven times before collapsing. Benny's brother opened the bar in 1947. Dad visited it in the late '70s. If it is still there I'd like to see it. Get your hat and I'll buy you a beer."

Late afternoon the bar was mostly empty. I could swear my client almost teared up looking at the memorabilia behind the bar.

We were sitting at the bar when a hand grabs me, spins me around, and sucker-punched me. Springing up, I caught my attacker with an uppercut sending him on to the nearest tables. Rosco, an 80-year-old man, came to my defense as two other men start to go at me. He broke his cane, one of the old fashion kind, a substantial piece of hickory, on one head. His partner punches Rosco in the gut and turns back on me.

The two are now holding me as Jimmy comes at me snarling. "You son of a bitch, you cost me a bundle. Time for payback!" After a couple of Jimmy's punches, the goon holding my left arm collapses, the one on the right is holding up his arm fending off the broken cane. Jimmy flees the premises and the two goons crawl out after him.

Someone is lifting me into a chair asking if I'm all right. It's not Rosco, he's still doubled over, gasping at the bar. My savior is a big dude, mid-forties, who looks like he is no stranger to barroom brawls. He introduces himself as Jeromy.

"You were a bit outnumbered partner, thought I'd help."

"Thanks," I say through a bloody lip.

"I'm surprised to see you here, either stupidity or balls. I'm no fan of Jimmy the Freak. Your takedown of him was brutal. Best entertainment I've had in years. He's a blowhard, stretching credibility defending himself on the radio."

We get Rosco back on his feet. The three of us claim one of the tables that's still upright and order drinks. Jeromy fills Rosco in on my recent history. Rosco has pretty much recovered. "This story will cap my visit to Benny's, sorry I couldn't do more," says Rosco, "but my cane was defective."

As Rosco and I are getting up to leave, I thank Jeromy again when he says, "I've taken some interest in you since the Monet and Jimmy story surfaced. I like your style. Have you ever thought about taking on a partner, someone to provide backup?"

"No, let me think about it. How can I get in contact with you?"

He gives me his cell number saying "I'm between jobs right now. I have a job offer in Jacksonville. They want my answer by Monday. If you're interested, call me by this weekend." We shook hands. Rosco and I walked out with Rosco muttering "Wait till I tell…".

Later at Helen's, over the mojito Helen provides on the house after seeing my battered face, I tell Michael about Jeromy's proposal.

"Interesting," he says. "Your caseload has picked up in the past few months, with one or two dicey moments … like today. Also, I wouldn't mind a little available muscle. I do get 'iffy' clients as you know." One example was the drug dealer's homies who threatened Michael's life when the dealer was convicted. "Let's take him on, on a trial basis. I'll cover half his salary."

The next morning I call Jeromy to my office to discuss his proposal. He arrives, almost on time. His first comment is, "Well you can't be accused of being a spendthrift. Where is your secretary?"

I explain my working relationship with the attorney downstairs, telling him we'll visit shortly if we come to terms. Salary is not an issue, he's happy with my first offer, eight hundred a week. The only stumbling block, he wants a desk. My office is much smaller than Michael's, but it does have an outer office, some would call it a cloakroom. It's my client waiting area if I ever have more than one client in the office at the same time. I agree to a small desk; he could be my receptionist I suggest. He starts to balk but then accepts with a grin. God help me, I'm thinking, "He's likely to scare off prospective clients."

Sensing my apprehension Jeromy says, "Not to worry George, I'm good with people."

We go down to Michael's office. He hits it off with Angelic. He's old enough to be her father. She flirts with him. Jokingly he tells her he's her counterpart in my office, but not as cute. Michael hears the voices and comes out.

Sitting in the inner office, Michael asks Jeromy about his background. "I grew up in a not-so-nice part of New York City" he starts. "Joined the army in time for Desert Storm. Was discharged in the early nineties ... honorable discharge mind you" he says with some pride. "I tried my hand at amateur boxing. Never was a contender, but I did okay. I worked as a security guard with Brinks. That was a good gig until some money went missing. I and my partner were let go, no charges were ever made, there was no evidence of our involvement. My last job was a bouncer at Maxime's until last month when I was asked to remove some rowdy customers. I may have been overly aggressive, two ended up in the hospital, with Maxime's footing the bill."

9: Lulabelle

Jeromy has been with me now for several months. I have to admit his intimidation factor has been useful when confronting reluctant deadbeats. His one drawback is speed on his feet. In a foot chase, he's useless, too bulky. As for his desk in the 'coat closet,' as he calls it, that's worked out well. Turns out he is very personable with distraught clients.

One small case that proved to be embarrassing walked through the front door shortly after Jeromy came on board. Jeromy greeted the elderly gentleman and after talking with him introduced Mr. Raileigh to me, "Mr. Raileigh from Topeka, Kansas. He owns a small manufacturing plant that makes car headlight assemblies. His son, Ralph, is enrolled at the College of Miami." It was one of the few schools that would accept him given his high school academics rated him at the bottom of the class. His problem, he likes to party. Now sending a party animal to Miami does not sound rational to me, but who am I to say? Anyway, the problem was Lulabelle.

Lulabelle is a cocktail waitress at the 'Bang Um Lounge.' Ralph was besotted with the curvy blond. It didn't matter that she was nearly ten years older than him. Earlier Ralph asked his father for his grandmother's wedding ring; he planned to propose and bring Lulabelle back to Topeka. She offered to help run the family business. Mr. Raileigh's tasking was simple -- break it up!

"I don't care what you do, I want her out of Ralph's life. I'll put five thousand down and you get another five when I see her backside."

"I think we can do that Mr. Raileigh," said Jeromy. "You just need to give us some details and we can get started."

After getting the details the man left. I turn to Jeromy, "We can do that -- how do you propose 'we' do that?"

"Easy, I'll go down to the Bang Um Lounge and scare the crap out of Lulabelle."

"That can put you in jail. Let's visit the lounge tonight and see what's what," I say.

At ten, we walk into the lounge and secure a couple bar stools. In the mirror over the bar, I'm watching the hostesses. There's one, a tall blond that looks like a 'Lulabelle.' Between serving other customers, she's flirting with a dork who doesn't look old enough to be in here.

"Jeromy don't turn but check out the booth, far side of the room, over your left shoulder. No, your other shoulder. I think we found Ralph. Here's the plan. You go over, make some crude comment to Lulabelle to get Ralph's dander up. He'll pop up to defend her honor, you two get into a minor scuffle, and you both get thrown out. Don't hurt him!"

My plan worked! I'll give Ralph credit for standing up to Jeromy. Jeromy outweighed him by a hundred pounds and was at least eight inches taller. He went after Jeromy like a wild man. When the bouncer tried to pull them apart, he started throwing punches at the bouncer.

After things settled down I moved to the now-vacated booth. The tall blond said with a come-on smile "What can I get you?"

We chatted for a bit between her rounds serving other customers. I asked what she was doing later. "What would you like me to be doing?" she responds. Needless to say, we hit it off, and by 2 a.m. I'm in her bed.

The phone is ringing, I grope for it. I'm groggy. The call goes to message saying "Miss La Bell, this is Betsy's Boutique, your order is ready to be picked up."

I sit up and look at my watch, it's mid-morning; I feel like I've been drugged. I look for my clothes, get dressed, and find my wallet and car keys are missing. Shit!!!

Quickly leaving Lulabelle's apartment I flag a passing taxi and have him take me to Betsy's Boutique. We get there and I find I have no money or credit card. Of course not, Lulabelle has my wallet. I tell the driver I'll be right out, and I sprint into the store.

Lulabelle is in the process of charging her purchases on my credit card; sees me enter the store, and starts shrieking, "He's after me! He's stalking me! Stop him!" and carrying on like someone in fear of her life.

The doorman rushes up and puts a hand on my shoulder, I turn to push him off. Continuing toward Lulabelle, the doorman unlashes his extendable baton and whacks me in the back of my knee. I go down, and the next thing I know, he's sitting on me. The salesclerk calls 911 and the uniforms are soon in the store slapping cuffs on me. Lulabelle has disappeared. I start to tell my story but no one is interested.

At the city jail, I get one phone call. I call Jeromy. He's not answering, he's in Michael's office flirting with Angelic.

Later that day I'm brought before an Arraignment Judge, a lady in her late fifties and with no sense of humor. I tell her I'm a PI, Lulabelle stole my wallet, and my partner has failed to respond.

"Mr. Basdakis, if that is who you are, you have a very implausible story. You are being charged with disorderly conduct, failure to pay a taxi fare, and if we can find the young lady you are allegedly stalking, with stalking. Guards take him back to his cell."

Luckily Michael was in the courtroom, his client was next on the Judge's docket.

"Your Honor, if I may address the court," he says. "This man is George Basdakis. He is a PI, and I employ him on occasion. I just checked with his partner, via text, and he confirmed Mr. Basdakis called earlier today, but he forgot to tell anyone."

The Judge calls me back, tells the guards to un-cuffed me, and directs me to have a seat while she hears the next case.

Later, in her chamber, she asks for the full story. On its completion, she looks at me, calls her clerk over, and tells him to prepare a warrant for Lulabelle's arrest. "Mr. Basdakis, I've been a Judge for close to twenty years now. I'm retiring next month. I seldom provide guidance where it's not sought, but I do have some advice for you, keep your zipper fasten when working a case."

10: The Scorpions

Michael has called us a few times over the past year to look into some aspects of his client's stories, hidden assets like Scott's offshore account mentioned above, fees from which are still covering my expenses. Jeromy and I have tracked down missing people for him, provided security for skittish clients, and other PI stuff. Michael has not balked at the five hundred per week he's paying to cover half of Jeromy's salary, "Money well spent" he says.

Michael's latest case was defending a motorcycle gang member on manslaughter charges. The gang known as the Scorpions has a long and violent relationship with another gang, the Angels.

'Killer,' the nickname of the Scorpions defendant, was charged with allegedly rigging 'Mutton Head's,' nickname of the deceased, motorcycle to freeze up when the bike's speed hit one hundred miles per hour. Earlier in the evening Killer was seen in the parking lot next to Mutton Head's bike. The witness to the supposed tampering admitted under cross-examination she had had several beers that evening. It was also shown she was an Angel's groupie.

The state's crime scene investigator determined that the bike's engine threw a rod as it exceeded 120 mph, recorded by one of those stationary speed cameras telling motorists how fast they're going. The posted speed on Rt. 1A, on that stretch, is 45 MPH. Mutton Head was thrown into oncoming traffic, traumatizing an elderly Canadian couple. The bike slid another thirty yards down the road, bursting into flames leaving very little for the reconstruction of the accident.

The court found Killer in contempt of court for his disregard of court etiquette but ruled Mutton Head's death was caused by his disregard for safety and excessive speed. Chalk up another win for Michael.

The day after the verdict I was across the street getting my morning coffee and croissant when five motorcyclists parked on the sidewalk outside our offices. The riders' jackets identified them as Angels. No good!

Pulling my iPhone out, I hit speed dial for Michael. "Michael you have some Angels coming up for a visit … no, not those kinds of angels."

Next, I called Jeromy. "Michael has some hostile visitors, meet me at the stairwell exit on the second floor."

By the time I get into the building, up the stairs, Jeromy is waiting. Two of the gang members are in Michael's office with three standing guard by the door. "I got the first two, you take the third guy" he yells as he rushes them, Jeromy easily takes his two down, leaving the third, the smallest, for me.

Bursting into Michael's office we find Angelic hiding behind her desk trying to get her new .38 out of the dealer's packaging. Bypassing her, we move into the inner office where two Angels have Michael on the floor, kicking the crap out of him. I grab Michael's Defense Attorney of the Year award, a heavy bronze statue of Lady Liberty, and plant it on the nearest skull. Jeromy's target is out cold on the floor.

As I'm calling 911, Jeromy is bent over Michael to assess the damage. He's moaning "Get those sons of bitches as he passes out."

"Check on Angelic," I tell Jeromy as we hear three bikes fire up and are halfway to the next block before I can look out the window.

A police cruiser arrives, lights flashing, followed by a rescue vehicle. As I'm explaining what happened to the uniformed officer, a detective struts in. I Ignore him as I turn to the paramedics. "How is he doing? How badly is he hurt? Which hospital are you taking him to?" And other pointless questions at this time.

Turning to the detective who is now showing signs of impatience at being ignored, he introduces himself as Detective Nathan Wrisley, and I have to start at the beginning.

Partway through my rendition of events, Wrisley stops me and asks, "Is this the shyster who got the manslaughter acquittal for that scumbag yesterday? Looks like he got what he deserves."

"We'll be filing assault charges. I'll come down to the station later."

"Don't rush?" the detective says with a grin, "I'm a slow typer, report won't be filed for a couple days."

Jeromy has Angelic sitting on the office sofa where she has regained her composure. Jeromy is asking about the gun. "Is that new? Do you know how to use it?"

"No" answers the girl, "Michael wanted a gun in the office and had me buy it last year."

As I'm leaving for the hospital I hear Jeromy saying, "I'll take you out to the shooting range next weekend and give you a few pointers."

At the hospital, I'm kept waiting for a couple of hours until Michael is moved from the emergency area to a private room.

I find his room, and walk in saying, "I've seen you looking better." He has three broken ribs and possible kidney damage; he has blood in his urine.

Michael's short-term goal is revenge. "Don't wait for the police" I say, "Detective Wrisley is not your supporter" and I relate my conversation with him.

41

"Okay, consider El Ojo Privado retained to get the bastards," he says as he drifts off into a morphine-induced slumber.

11: The Angels

Back in Michael's office Jeromy and I help Angelic clean up the mess. I give Angelic an update on Michael's condition. "You should go home, nothing more to do here. Michael is at St. Mary's Hospital, room 303. Talk with him tomorrow to see what he wants you to do for the rest of the week. Tell him we are working on his case."

As she leaves Jeromy is saying "Let's go bash some heads." He wants to tackle this head-on. I, on the other hand, want to be a bit more devious.

"Sit tight," I tell Jeromy as I go into Michael's office and rifle through his files looking for Killer's folder. Finding it, I page through it until I find who retained Michael. Stan Wojciehowicz. His contact information indicates he's the President of the Scorpions Motorcycle Club. I write down the club's address and collect Jeromy on my way out.

"Where're we going?" he fusses.

We find the old warehouse listed as the club's command center. There, fifteen, maybe twenty bikes are parked in the delivery area. "You sure you want to go in there?" Jeromy asks.

"You can stay in the car if you feel threatened," I say, knowing he'll be on my heels going in.

Inside we find the area is decently lit, we can see everyone. There are two pool tables in the middle of the space with lights hanging over them, a well-stocked bar at the far end managed by a tough-looking amazon with a mohawk haircut, and a collection of tables along the wall, most occupied.

With the exception of a pool ball falling into a pocket, quiet. A large imposing figure lays down his pool cue and asks in a very quiet, but threatening voice, "Who the hell are you?"

"I'm George Basdakis, I work with Michael Zych." The mention of Michael's name relaxed the tension in the room. "Michael is in the hospital. A crew from the Angels beat the crap out of him this morning for defending Killer."

Stan looked threatening before, but now he's volcanic. "What happened?"

I tell him the story, from my coffee and croissant to Detective Nathan Wrisley's final comment. Stan invites us over to a table, gets us a beer, and rhetorically asks "Okay what are we going to do?"

Killer, who was standing by the wall says, "We can take them out tonight; baseball bats and Molotov cocktails ..."

Speaking up I say, "Not being a member of your club, if I may, I have a suggestion. The police will have a stakeout on the Angels after this morning's events. Let the dust settle. In a few days, the police will go away, the Angels will let their guard down … and then hit them."

Stan mulls this over. "You make some good points. We'll get them next week."

***

The following Wednesday, make that early Wednesday morning, Detective Wrisley is pounding on my door "Where were you last night?" I know you are part of this and I'm going to nail your ass!"

Half asleep I ask, "What's got your shorts in a knot?"

"Don't play coy with me, you bastard. The Angels' building was firebombed about eight last night resulting in three deaths and a dozen or more in the hospital. Like I said, where were you last night?"

"The opera?"

He loses it, ordering the uniforms to cuff me and take me downtown.

After spending the next three hours in an empty interrogation room, Wrisley finally makes an appearance. "I've pulled your record. I see you've been arrested for stalking. Interesting. Moved on to arson now I see. What kind of sadistic bastard are you?"

"Talk," he says.

"Phone," I say.

After fifteen minutes of repetition, he gets up in frustration and tells the guard to let me make a phone call. I call Michael's office; he's been in for a few hours a day recently. Angelic answers. I tell her what's happened and where I am. "Tell Jeromy, and if Michael is able, I need his help."

After a short bathroom break, I'm back in the interrogation room. Two more hours pass before Wrisley reappears. He's pissed; "Your shyster is here, you're free to go." Michael is in the hallway, in obvious pain. Wrisley wouldn't even allow him to sit.

Jeromy is in the lobby, he drove, and he's still in the dark. His first question is "What the hell happened?"

I tell him. Back in Michael's office, Michael makes some phone calls. He repeats back to us what he's just been told.

"It appears about seven last night nights the Angels clubhouse was firebombed. The main door was barricaded with one of those large commercial trash bins. There were three confirmed deaths and numerous burn victims. Two nearby buildings were also partially destroyed. All security cameras were taken out, probably by pellet guns. Given the remote location of the site, there were no witnesses, or more likely, witnesses that wanted to come forward."

12: I Know Nothhhhhing

Michael's cell phone rings with that annoying 'Cavalry Bugle Charge.' Its Stan. "Michael we need to talk."

"Not on the phone, meet George at the City Library in an hour, by yourself," Michael says and disconnects.

He calls in Angelic. "Angelic, draw up an agreement between me and the Scorpion Motorcycle Club, inclusive for all members as of today, for legal representation. I'll sign it now and have a signature block for Stan Wojciehowicz."

"George, you meet with Stan at the library and get his signature. We need this on file before the shit hits the fan. Tell Stan and his people to lay low, it's only a matter of time before the police start pulling them in. Tell him to give them my name and Angelic, print up a sheet of labels with my name and number. George, have Stan give one of these labels to each of his people. Emphasize no one says anything!!"

I'm on my way to the library, using Angelic's car and taking a circuitous route to foil any tail Detective Wrisley may have placed on me. Finding the city library is my first challenge. I haven't been in a library since I visited the medieval section in college. I find it on West Flagler Street. There is a Harley parked in a handicapped space; Stan is already here. I find him sitting in the main reading room and suggest we move to one of the cubicles on the side.

"I want to talk with my lawyer, not you" were Stan's first words.

"And pigs want to fly."

"You know the Angel's clubhouse was firebombed last night. Wrisley dragged me to the police station and was questioning me at three this morning. Michael got me out at eleven. It's only a matter of time before they come after you. Michael prepared this agreement where you retain him to be your, and the Scorpion's, attorney. Sign it. Also here are labels for all your club members with Michael's name and number. We expect the police to pick some of you up. Tell them to memorize Sergeant Schultz's line, 'I know nothhhhhing' and call Michael. Questions?"

"We didn't do it!" Stan nearly shouts.

"Keep it down, don't draw attention to us" I hiss.

"We didn't do it; our hit was planned for Thursday night. As a matter of fact, most of us were in West Palm Beach Tuesday evening at a Gathering of the Bikes show put on by the Harley dealership. We have witnesses."

"That's good. Okay if you didn't firebomb them, who did?"

"I don't know," Stan says. "The drug cartel? It's rumored they were moving drugs up the East Coast. They also had some contact with the mob moving hot cars. Either could have done it."

13: Anthony Nardi

Back in Michael's office, we discuss Stan's denial. Michael wants Jeromy to go to West Palm Beach to verify the Scorpion's alibi. Pending confirmation, we will be left with two possible suspects, the mob with the car theft ring, or the Guerra Drug Cartel.

We think the cartel is the more likely given their violent history. The Guerra Drug Cartel is centered in Venezuela and is thought to be, no let's be more specific, is connected to the Venezuelan Government. It is one of the country's major sources of foreign currency since the current regime wrecked the country's oil economy.

"Jeromy," Michael says, "After you visit West Palm Beach, visit your old haunts in Jacksonville and see what rumors you can pick up on the Angels. I think they have an affiliated club there."

"George, you should look into the car theft ring. Rumors in the courthouse suggest Anthony Nardi is Miami's head mobster, but nothing has ever been linked to him. Nardi has cousins with the New York mob, one or two serving time. A connection between Nardi and the Angels has always been iffy. He's hard to find, you'll need to hunt him down."

It's late in the afternoon, "Happy Hour beckons" I say. Jeromy begs off, he wants to leave for Jacksonville now. There is a coastal shuttle service that can have him there by seven. Some of his old buddies up there have a standing Friday night party and he says that is a good place to start. He will hit West Palm on his way back.

Angelic also declines. There is a family birthday party for her baby brother; she needs to attend.

"Okay just the two of us," Michael says, "How's Helen's?"

***

Saturday, I start my search for Anthony Nardi in earnest. Where better to start than with Helen's third cousin, Peter Stavros? Pete is an elderly gentleman, recently retired from the Miami Herald. For the past fifty years, he's been the paper's lead crime reporter. Helen suggested him as a source last night after Michael and I used her as a sounding board.

Following Helen's directions, I find Pete's bungalow. Actually, it is a nice three-bedroom home in a new retirement community north of the city. Peter, a tall man with a towel wrapped around his waist, comes to the door after my repeatedly ringing the bell and knocking on the door.

"Sorry for the delay, I didn't hear you at first. We're outback with the grandkids, playing in the pool. You must be George Basdakis, my cousin called this morning asking if I would see you. Come in."

"Thanks for taking the time," I say as I enter the foyer. He leads me through the house to one of the bedrooms which has been converted into an office. The walls are covered with framed news clippings. The shelf at the back of his desk is loaded with awards. There is a computer driving two screens, a large printer-fax-copy machine in the corner: and an old fashion landline telephone on the desk.

"I've been retired for close to a year now but I still like to stay in touch with the city. Helen said you're a PI looking for information on the local mob. If I may say so, that is an unhealthy undertaking. But, before we start would you care for coffee or a soda?"

I decline, thanking him for the offer, and then launch into my story starting with the trial finding the Scorpion gang member innocent of manslaughter, the Angel's retribution attack on Michael, and cumulating in the firebombing of the Angel's clubhouse resulting in three deaths.

"My police contacts have been helping me follow that story. If I were still working, I'd be all over this. Are the Scorpions guilty? I don't think so, too obvious. I'd dig deeper."

"Stan Wojciehowicz, the Scorpion's president says it wasn't them. He claims club members were in West Paul Beach the night it happened. When I asked Stan who did it he claimed not to know, suggesting it could have been the Guerra Drug Cartel or the local mob. It's rumored the Angels were moving product up the East Coast for the cartel. Perhaps there was a falling out. It's also rumored the Angels were providing security for the mob moving hot cars. Either could have done it."

"Both are logical candidates," says Peter, "but I bet the police are focused on the Scorpions, whom I'm guessing, hired you to prove otherwise."

"So obvious," I say with a grin. "We think they are innocent, that is why we have taken their case."

"We?"

"Michael Zych, my partner and the attorney that got the original acquittal. As I said, we think the Scorpions are innocent and are leaning toward the drug cartel as the guilty party. We have one of our people working on that possibility."

"But, we are not ignoring the mob's possible involvement. Were the Angels providing security services? Did this relationship go sideways? Who is Anthony Nardi and how do I find him? That's my focus today."

Peter thinks for a moment and finally says, "Nardi is not to be trifled with, he's dangerous. He's been on my radar for the past decade, ever since the mob upped their presence in south Florida. I've never been able to get that much on him. The best I can tell you is it is believed he uses an old warehouse by the docks."

After a few more questions I thank Peter for his time.

My next stop is a police snitch Michael knows and has used on occasion. In the morning I find him in a café in Little Havana. At first, he was reluctant to talk to me. As he gets up to leave, I mention Michael sent me.

"Why didn't you say so, I do Mr. Z a favor every now and then. What did you say your name was?"

"I'm George Basdakis. I'm a PI and am working for Michael on this case. Come sit back down, can I get you another coffee?"

"No, I'm good, what do you want to know?"

"Have you ever heard of Anthony Nardi?"

The snitch pales a bit and says "No, I don't know Tony."

"That's a shame," I say as I finger a roll of franklins. Michael was willing to pay for your information, but, if you don't know Nardi, you don't know him." I start to get up....

"Wait," says the snitch as he eyes the franklins. "I might have been a bit hasty. If I tell you anything about Tony, it's just between you and me right?"

"Definitely."

"He likes the Tropicana Club. He's hot for one of the dancers, Lily I think her name is."

I peel off two bills and thank him for his time and tell him I'll remember him to Mr. Z.

14: Regrouping

Tuesday morning we're in Michael's office. Michael's focus is on the expense report submitted by El Ojo Privado.

"George, these expenses you and Jeromy are claiming are outrageous. Ten-dollar lattes for a snitch, reimbursement for enough gas to get you to Atlanta and back. And you Jeromy, claiming expenses for first-class Coastal Airways tickets, an airline that advertises one price for any seat," he yells as he crumples my expense report and tosses it toward the waste basket – and misses.

After a deep breath, "Okay, what have you got?"

I report on my limited luck in tracking down Nardi. I paraphrase my conversation with Peter Stavros. "I think he's a good source; you might want to add him to your contact list." Then I recap my meeting with the snitch. "I was thinking of inviting Angelic, as cover, to join me visiting the Tropicana this weekend."

"Forget that; keep her out of this!" Michael snaps. What do you have Jeromy?"

"Starting with West Palm Beach, the Scorpions were there. There were fifteen or twenty Scorpions there. They were almost arrested for causing a disturbance at the wet tee-shirt contest. Young ladies, if you will, ran around the showroom as bikers pelted them with water-filled balloons. Stan grabbed one, tossed her over his shoulder, and was leaving when security busted him. Their alibi is good."

"Now, I think I hit paydirt at Jacksonville. An old buddy told me about the Angels running cocaine up to New York for the Guerra Drug Cartel. The Jacksonville chapter was not involved, other than providing limited security between Jacksonville and the North Carolina-Virginia state line. They'd run a few bikes ahead of the drug couriers to sniff out police roadside stakeouts. Last spring, two outriders disappeared along with the Angel couriers when they diverted to the coastal route. Rumor had it that the Virginia State Police were waiting for them at the state line. Anyway, they all disappeared in the Great Dismal Swamp, along with a quarter million in cartel product."

"To make a long story short, it's believed the Angels took the cocaine; the Jacksonville bikers were never heard from again. The couriers crept back to Miami. A few months later, the Angels brokered a drug deal with a dealer from New Orleans."

"The cartel was not amused. Two of my contacts, not the bikers, think they saw Castro Gutierrez in the Jacksonville airport a few days after news of the New Orleans drug deal started circulating. Castro is a Venezuelan hitman. A week later, the Angels' clubhouse is firebombed."

***

Three weeks later, my old friend Detective Nathan Wrisley arrests Stan and his two lieutenants for murder. At their arraignment, Michael attempts to have the charges thrown out, but the Judge won't have it; won't even listen to Michael's argument. They are held with no bail.

Michael's gym membership pays off. Michael gets wind that the grand jury is meeting to consider charges against the Scorpions. After a vicious round on the handball court, Michael broaches the pending hearing with the prosecutor handling the case.

"You know better than that, Zych; I can't discuss grand jury deliberations."

"I know; I don't want you to say anything. Just listen. The Angels were running drugs for the Guerra Drug Cartel. A major shipment went missing. Shortly after that, the Angels were selling cocaine to a known dealer from New Orleans. This was followed by the arrival of Castro Gutierrez in Jacksonville, a noted Venezuelan hitman. The defendants have an iron-tight alibi. They were in West Palm Beach at the time of the fire. But I'm sure all this is in Detective Wrisley's report."

Two days later, Stan and company are released. Michael's police contact reported Wrisley was put on a week's suspension, without pay, for shoddy work.

Not to let my tracking of Anthony Nardi go to waste, my curiosity peeked, I decided to visit the Tropicana. I invite Jeromy to join me. He's not interested and has other plans for the night.

15: Negotiation

Friday night, eleven-thirty, I pull into the Tropicana parking lot. It's full, I'm forced to park on the median strip between the nightclub and the adjacent strip mall. I find a seat at the bar. The room is packed with old men, showgirls, and tourists. I find myself out of place. When I order my second scotch and soda, I ask the bartender, "Is Lily working tonight?"

He looks at me and turns to serve another customer. I lay a fifty on the bar, it gets his attention, and as he retrieves it says, "See the tall brunette in the red costume? That's Lily."

Lily is hovering around a table with three middle-aged men. Two are on the bulky side, the third is bald and skinny. Lily is slipping onto the third's lap. That must be Anthony, I'm thinking. Using my cell phone, I discreetly take his picture. Okay, now, what? I sip my drink, order a third, and formulate a plan. Maybe I can follow them.

I'm on my fourth scotch and soda when they get up to leave. I follow from a distance. I see Nardi get into a new Cadillac Eldorado in the parking lot. I didn't see his two buddies as they came up behind me, one punching me in the kidneys. I gasp for breath. The numbing effect of the alcohol doesn't help. Each grabs an arm and drags me to the Cadillac. Nardi opens the door, "Put him in; I want to talk to him."

Still in pain, I find myself sitting next to the man I've been seeking.

"George Basdakis isn't it," Nardi says. "You've been asking about me for the past week. What do you want?"

Surprised he knows my name, I keep a straight face and tell him my story. "I'm a PI, and you were a potential suspect in the firebombing of the Angel's clubhouse. Suspicion has now shifted to the Guerra Drug Cartel. The police are focused on a Venezuelan hit man named Castro."

"And how did you tie me to the firebombing?" he asks

"It's rumored the Angels provide security services for some of your operations."

"What operations?"

"Transport of stolen cars," I say.

He laughs and, taking my phone, tells me to get out. His parting words were, "It's healthy to mind your own business."

***

Three weeks later, one of Nardi's bulky friends comes to my office. Jeromy and the 'Bulk,' my new nickname for the man, have a staring contest to see who waivers first. I give credit to Jeromy; outweighed by at least fifty pounds and a bulge under the man's jacket, Jeromy stood his ground.'

"Mr. Nardi wants to talk with you – now!" the Bulk said,

I'm curious; I agree to go with him. "Jeromy, lock the office; we are invited out on a social call."

"No, just you," the Bulk snaps.

Well, in that case, you will just have to tell Mr. Nardi you failed. Jeromy comes with me, or I stay put."

He makes a quick cell call. "Okay, he can come," the Bulk concedes, glaring at Jeromy.

It was at this point Tony engaged El Ojo Privado to locate the missing hundred thousand dollars.

Jump forward one week.

It was about a week between my initial meeting with Nardi, not counting the conversation in his Cadillac and the persuasive suggestion that I deliver Jeromy to the warehouse. I had an inkling as to where the meeting was going. I knew Jeromy had lifted the cash. Expecting the worst, I enlisted Stan for a little backup.

So there we were in Nardi's warehouse, Jeromy tied to a chair and Nardi telling me I was free to go.

"Tony, if I can call you Tony," I said, "the Scorpions have your brother. If you hurt Jeromy, they hurt Alfredo. Now I admit Jeremy was a bit greedy, but look at him, set money in front of him … he's tempted. Tell you what, I'll waive my fee, you let Jeromy go, and Stan will bring you Alfredo. We're all happy."

Tony glares at me, waives to the Bulk to untie Jeromy, and says, "You got balls. I got a deal for you and the Scorpions. I need security for my car business if they are up to it. Ever since the Angels were burned out, my operation has been at a standstill. They can work for me ... and I'll keep your fee."

"You need to talk to Stan; I don't manage their affairs. Let me call him, and you can discuss your business arrangement."

When Jeromy and I left the warehouse, Tony and Stan were talking.

16: Dealing

I visit the Scorpions' hideaway every two or three weeks. Michael has managed a few misdemeanors for them that resulted in court hearings. I've provided some investigative support. Tonight Stan was in a talkative mood, or was it the alcohol, didn't matter; he was talking about Tony's operation.

"We've taken some fine cars up to Jacksonville, load them onto Tony's ship. He's getting cars from all up and down the East Coast. The ship leaves full of cars. Tony is shipping stolen cars to his friends in South America."

"How many cars are on the ship?" I ask, "and is the ship empty when it comes back?"

Stan thinks for a minute, "Probably about a hundred fifty cars. I've never seen the ship return, but I think it's empty. Why do you want to know all this?"

"Just curious, shooting the breeze."

"If you're smart, you won't be snooping into Mr. Nardi's business. It's not healthy."

The next morning I'm talking with Jeromy. "Sounds like Tony has a nice aftermarket car business. Do you know anything about it?" I ask.

"There are old rumors of the mob shipping hot cars out of Jacksonville and Savanna, but I don't know anything specific."

"Could you visit your old friends in Jacksonville and see what you can find out? What's the name of the ship? Where does it go?" I ask.

"Sure, I'm on the clock, right?" he responds.

"Yes, I'm paying, not Michael, so don't pad your expenses!"

The following Monday, Jeromy is back. "The ship's name is the *Fada do Carro,* Portuguese for the 'Car Fairy.' It has Brazilian registry. It's a small ship capable of carrying up to two hundred cars. I talked to two of the crew members. You'll find their bar tab, and by the way, they drink like sailors in my expense report. They normally deliver the cars to Porto Alegre in Brazil. They claim there is a sophisticated setup to receive the cars."

"Were they able to name any contacts?" I ask, expecting a negative answer.

"Do they pick up any cargo on the way back to Jacksonville?"

"No, and no."

"Thanks, you did good."

***

Thinking over what I've learned, a plan starts to come to me. I call Michael and tell him I'm going on vacation, will be back in a week or so. I tell Jeromy the same.

On my way home to pack, I called United Airways and booked a flight to Porto Alegre. I have to change planes in Rio de Janeiro. My twelve-hour flight gives me time to do a little internet sleuthing. I find that the *Fada do Carro*is is a Brazilian ship registered to Coastal Shipping, headquartered in Porto Alegre. The CEO is Gustaf Kohl. I copy down his contact information.

One of the benefits of north-south travel, there is no time lag. I got a good night's sleep and was at Coastal Shipping at nine the following day. I ask to see Senior Kohl.

The receptionist, in good English, asks, "Do you have an appointment?"

"No, this is a surprise visit," and playing a hunch, say, "Anthony Nardi sent me."

The lobby receptionist calls the CEO's receptionist. After an exchange in Portuguese, the young lady says I can go up; pointing at the elevator bank, you want the twenty-third floor.

Gustaf is waiting when I get off the elevator. "I hope Mr. Nardi is well," he starts. "I wasn't expecting a visit. What can I do for you?"

I want to talk about our operation here. We ship cars to you every few weeks, and the Fada do Carrois returns to the US empty. I have an idea that might be profitable for you and Mr. Nardi.

"Does Mr. Nardi know about this idea? Gustaf asks.

"No, not yet; I'm just working out some of the details."

"And the idea is?"

"We have a border crisis in the States; people just streaming across our southern border. You may have heard of this."

"I have but can't understand it. Why do your leaders keep your borders open? It makes no sense."

"The Mexican cartels," I continue, "are making a fortune. I'm thinking we might be able to cash in on this. Many of these illegals come from Venezuela, Argentina, Cuba, and some from Brazil. Many pay up to ten thousand dollars per person to smugglers. Their journey takes them several weeks, through the Panamanian jungles, then an iffy trip north. Then they may spend weeks in custody once they reach America. My idea, the Fada do Carrois can bring one hundred two hundred migrants, maybe more, back on return trips. Making us a million dollars per trip."

"Interesting. This idea would require someone in Brazil to coordinate this program?" Gustaf is pondering aloud.

"Yes, and I expect some compensation would be provided for these efforts and reimbursement for support costs. Unlike cars, people need food, water, and some rudimentary facilities on the ship. We'd be selling a relatively quick trip to the States and a safe trip."

"My question to you, Señor, can you make it work at this end?"

"I need to discuss this with some *parceiros,* my partners. How long will you be here?"

"As long as you need. I'll call you tomorrow."

Two nights later, Gustaf invited me to dinner with his partners. They are sold on the idea.

***

Back in Miami, I'm selling the idea to Tony. Gustaf's call totally blindsided him, and he was ranting and raving when the Bulk escorted me into the warehouse.

"Take a breath, Tony, sit down. I'm giving you a deal that should net you an extra $700, $800 thousand for each trip the Fada do Carrois makes."

"What do you know about the Fada do Carrois?" he snaps.

"Sit down and listen," I say, "or I'll take my idea to your cousins in New York. Yes, I know about them."

After some talk, Tony comes around.

"What do we do with illegals when they get here," he asks.

"Put them on buses and send them to Atlanta, Washington DC, New York, wherever you want," I respond. "Stan's people can drive some of the buses, and your friends in New York can drive some of the buses. These illegals will blend in with the ones the Government is shipping around the country."

Tony's sold. Over the next few days, he sells the idea to his cousins in New York. They decide a face-to-face is needed, so I'm brought along more or less for show 'n tell. The New York 'Don' wants me to coordinate the Brazilian end. My compensation will not be inconsequential he tells me.

Over the six months, I spend more than half my time in Porto Alegre. Gustaf has set me up in one of the new high-rise condos. I don't tell Michael or Jeromy what I'm doing. I tell them it's just a sideline and will tell them if it works out. Jeromy is left in charge of El Ojo Privado.

17: Porto Alegre

"Gustaf, this is a great condo overlooking the historic district with the dock area just behind. I'm looking forward to my stay in Porto Alegre."

"This is one of the newest condos in the city. I pulled some strings to get you this unit. Now I have to get back to the office. We will meet tomorrow to discuss our new *esteira rolante* venture. This gives you a free day."

"Esteira rolante?" I say with a puzzled look.

"That's Portuguese for people mover," Gustaf explains with a smile.

"Would it be possible to get a tour of our used car operation? I might get some ideas for our meeting."

Okay, I don't see the harm in that. Let me call one of my men, Rafael Moreno. He'll meet you here in an hour.

True to his word, the condo concierge called an hour later, "Señor Murphy, you have a visitor in the lobby, a Señor Moreno."

"Tell him I will be right down, thank you."

Rafael was a middle-aged man slightly shorter than me, and as a plus, he spoke good English.

"Señor Murphy, Señor Kohl said you would like a tour of our car processing facilities."

"Rafael, please call me George. I expect we will be working together over the next year. Tell me about your time with Coastal Shipping."

"I have been with the company for fifteen years but was only brought into this part of the business two years ago. I was initially reluctant, given the nature of the work. Still, it pays good, better than working the docks, and as a benefit, I get a nice car, a Ford Explorer. Where would you like to start?"

"Let's start at the dock where the ship unloads its cargo and follow a make-believe car through the system."

Down at the docks, the dock usually used by the 'Car Fairy' is empty. Rafael tells me how the cars are offloaded and loaded onto car carriers. They are taken to our prep facility north of the city, next to the rail line."

"Why a prep facility ?"

"Most of the cars have damaged steering columns. The thief frequently had to smash the ignition key mechanism to free the steering column lock and hot wire the car. Damage is usually minimal and can be repaired quickly. Some cars have minor body damage, and all the cars need new key fobs. We also change the VINs."

We arrive at a large warehouse with a good size parking lot that is half full of late-model cars, a hundred or more. Walking into the warehouse, I see a modern garage with multiple bays. Ten or fifteen cars are being worked on. Walking deeper into the building, there is a body shop. The next stop is the out-processing area, where key fobs are made, and new VINs assigned. We pass through the detailing area where cars are washed, buffed, vacuumed, and made like new. Finally, we entered the showroom. We are greeted by a 'salesman.' "Why are all used car salesmen worldwide sleazy?" I ask myself.

"How long do the cars sit here?" I ask Rafael.

"Not long. Buyers can come here and select a car, just like any used car lot. Once a week, we will ship fifty by rail to Rio de Janeiro. Monthly we will send a car carrier to Brasília, but those cars are specifically ordered. We have 100 percent turnover every six weeks. Turnover is balanced with new car arrivals."

"How many people work here in car processing?" I ask.

"I've never asked, but I would guess twenty to twenty-five. That's not counting the drivers, but many of those are part-time."

The day is young, so I asked Rafael if he could give me a quick tour of the city and point out some good restaurants and night spots. He's happy to have a little free time and we spend the next few hours cruising the city streets.

As we drive, he tells me the history of the city. "Porto Alegre was founded in 1772 by Manuel Sepúlveda and first populated with immigrants from the Azores. In the later part of the 19th century and the early 20th century, a large number of immigrants from Italy and Germany arrived. In the late 1940s, Coastal Shipping was founded by WWII German refugees. Gustaf Kohl's father was one. There is a rumor that Nazi looted gold provided the seed money. Senior Kohl doesn't like to talk about that; please don't mention I told you."

We ended the day with dinner at an excellent German restaurant, Die Kleine Heidelberg. I thanked Rafael for the tour and reaffirmed my lips were sealed regarding any rumors.

18: Planning

I arrived at Coastal Shipping's board room at the prescribed time, ten a.m. Gustaf's secretary escorts me in, pointing out coffee and pastries on the side table. Gustaf is sitting at the head of the table; three other board members are present.

"Good morning George. Gentlemen, this is George Basdakis, Mr. Nardi's man. The esteira rolante venture is his idea. If it is successful, we all benefit; if it fails ... well, then it's his head. Just kidding George, we have a winner here," Gustaf says with a smile.

"Let me introduce you to the team. The man to my left is Luiz Ramalho. He will manage the refitting of the Fada do Carro to accommodate passengers. Next to you is Carlos Dias, and beside him is Higor da Silva. They are our recruiters; they'll find passengers."

Gustaf turns to Luiz, asking what he has planned for the ship.

"Moving people is different from moving cars. People are more finicky. George's plan, as I understand it, calls for the ship to handle up to two hundred migrants for a three or four-day voyage. We need to retrofit the ship to provide eating, bathroom, and sleeping facilities."

Luiz projects a diagram of the Fada do Carro on the wall showing the uppermost deck, two lower decks where cars are carried, and the steerage area. "I will install refrigeration units in the steerage area to keep perishables, but the primary food will be boxed ready-to-eat meals. We will install two tanks: one for fresh water and the other a waste holding tank. The waste tank can be flushed at sea. We will install a small galley on the lower car deck, mostly microwave units, for food prep. A dumbwaiter will be installed, connecting the galley with the food storage area.

"Where will they sleep," I ask.

"On the deck. I will have air mattresses, blankets, and pillows. These items will be kept in steerage for southbound trips and brought out for northbound trips. Not a luxury liner, but better than spending a night or two in the Darién Gap."

Luiz concludes by noting the proposed permanent additions to the ship will only take two car spaces.

Turning to Carlos, Gustaf asks, "How do we get passengers?"

"Higor and I have been busy. Our first thought was to get Venezuelan refugees. We visited Boa Vista, a refugee collection point on our border with Venezuela. Migrants there are mostly farmers and small shopkeepers, non-have two coins to rub together. Next, we went to Medellín to talk with the Columbian cartel. Their best offer was to screen migrants for those who can pay or have access to money and fly them to us in old DC-3s, only two thousand a head, American. That cuts our profits, but it's a starting point until word of mouth starts generating customers."

"That's disappointing," I say. "How can we market this operation in the Middle East, Pakistan, or Africa?" I ask. "Current FOX News reports that immigrants from over thirty countries have been wading across the Rio Grande, daily. Carlos, Higor, you have to up your game."

As I'm berating our recruitment team, a middle-aged man enters the room, Gustaf greets him, "Juan, I was wondering where you were."

"George, this is Juan Reyes; he's in charge of security. Last year we had a major security shakeup. Our old head of security, Juan Hernandez, was arrested by the *Policia Federal*."

"We have a long-standing relationship with the branch of the Federal Police that handles maritime issues. That idiot Hernandez cut our seasonal 'gifts' to key police officials by one-third and pocketed the money. At a Christmas party, Colonel Faria, the branch head, asked about Coastal Shipping's contributions to the police retirement fund. When I found out what that idiot did, I worked with Faria to get a conviction. Juan Hernandez is now serving a twenty-year sentence for bribing an official."

We found Juan Reyes in San Paulo working for one of our larger competitors, the *Importadores de carros*. We convinced him to join our team. An unexpected outcome was the *Car Importers*, the group's name in English, wanted to join us as a subsidiary. They import most of their inventory from Europe. This alliance has worked out well.

"How do they get their 'inventory' to San Paulo?" I ask. "If by ship, does the ship have any capacity to carry people?"

"That's an interesting question," says Gustaf. Carlos, look into it."

***

Six months later, the esteira rolante venture is running like clockwork. The Columbia cartel provides a small number of 'rich' migrants, mostly Indian and Pakistani. These migrants are charged a premium rate for transportation to the US's East Coast. Most pay with gold jewelry.

The Car Importers provide a similar number of people, mostly from Syria, Iraq, and Afghanistan. Again these migrants are charged a premium rate; payment is mostly in old, well-worn one-hundred-dollar bills.

The bulk of our cargo is walk-ins from Africa, the Caribbean, and South American countries. They are charged a steerage rate, usually funded by their families. Word-of-mouth advertising is working.

The demand for people smuggling is stressing our resources. The Car Fairy is now carrying five hundred bodies on each return trip. Projections suggest we will move seven to ten thousand illegals per year. Small potatoes compared to the southern border inflow, but profitable to us – twenty-five to forty million a year.

Tony is being pressured to ship more cars to Porto Alegre just to accommodate a demand for increasing northbound human traffic. The Mob's Don is being pressured to start another 'car export' operation in Boston.

As demand grows, I wonder how we can get more revenue with the same resources. Can we offer a premium service?

I share some ideas with Gustaf, he likes them.

I'm off to Medellín to meet with the Columbian drug cartel.

***

I hitch a ride on one of the DC-3s returning to Columbia. I previously contacted the cartel, and they have a team on the ground to meet me. Carlos and Miguel greet me at the small regional airport, the Olaya Herrera Airport. Taxiing to the terminal, I see three other DC-3s, the cartel's I assume. I only have a small carry-on, so we are quickly on our way.

"Senor Guzman is wondering about the purpose of your visit," says Carlos. "Shipment of migrants to Porto Alegre is proving most beneficial. Gustaf recently expressed pleasure in our cooperation."

"We are very pleased with the arrangement. I am here to talk with Senor Guzman about an idea I have to make us all happier," I say.

"What idea is that?" asks Miguel.

"You want me to tell you before I tell Senior Guzman? That sounds like a ballsy move on your part, perhaps a career-defining move," I respond with some seriousness.

It's a short ride up into the hills surrounding Medellín. We enter a gated community, *Mirador del Poblado*. Guzman's compound is twice the size of nearby homes. I'm escorted into a large room; Guzman is seated on a leather sofa overlooking a large bank of picture windows that provide a panoramic view of the city.

"Please have a seat Mr. Basdakis," he says, pointing to an overstuffed chair that shares the view. "This is a beautiful view of the city," he says, "perhaps one of the best."

"Gustaf tells me that esteira rolante, people mover, was your idea. Is that right?"

"Yes."

"A brilliant idea; what can I do for you today?" he asks.

"Let's make it better," I start. "You may know that we are swamped with business. I'm looking for ways to increase profits, but we can't move more people. We're maxed out. I want to put a filter in at your end. I'm proposing that you restrict passage to those who can pay twenty thousand dollars per head, up from the current ten. And, of course, we share with you, your payment would increase by 10 percent."

77

"You increase your take by a hundred percent and only give me ten. That hardly seems fair," says Guzman.

"Let me enhance my plan a bit, and then we can talk about a 25 percent increase. I propose you market a VIP migrant service. The higher cost will buy luxury services. We will house them in a better holding area, give them preferred treatment on the ship, and provide a more personalized relocation service when they arrive in the States. Your transport of migrants will be more akin to a commercial airline, not cattle cars."

"You want to turn my operation into a luxury travel service?" laughs Guzman.

"Yes, and as feedback on the new 'luxury travel services' reaches families on the Indian subcontinent, your business will grow."

Guzman is sitting there, contemplating my sales pitch.

"Let me add one more inducement. We have more people seeking passage than we can accommodate. I propose we load returning planes with them, and you can move them up through Panama for your normal fee. And we won't charge you anything for these bodies."

Guzman continues contemplating my sales pitch and then breaks into a big smile, "I like it. We can do it for a 25 percent increase. Carlos, get with our people and tell me how you will implement our friend's plan."

19: Home

It's been almost nine months since I've been in my office. I find Jeromy at my desk. He does a doubletake when he looks up from his racing form. "Well, look who's finally back. Where've you been?" he says as he jumps up. "Michael has been asking about you every week or so, but in the past few months, he's asking less."

Jeromy and I go down to the second floor and surprise Angelic. "Your still here? I thought you'd have a better-paying job by now," I say to her. "Is Michael in?" She nods yes.

"Call him and tell him there's a process server looking for him," I say.

The call is made, and moments later, Michael appears with a worried look, sees me, and breaks into a toothy grin, "Where the hell have you been George?"

"That I can't tell you yet, but let's close-up shop; it's almost happy hour. Helen's is calling."

Helen gave me a big hug when we arrived, "Where have you been George" were her first words.

"Michael sent me on a secret mission," I say. She looks at Michael, and he shrugs, shaking his head saying, "George is fantasizing; he was lost in Little Havana."

The next day I visited Tony. The Bulk is there to escort me in.

"George, that was a fantastic idea you launched. He apologized for ever doubting. We are pulling in millions from people moving."

"How are Stan's people doing busing our immigrants to their final destinations?" I ask. "Each delivery must require ten or fifteen buses."

He has it under control. We rotate deliveries between three ports. Buses are staged near the receiving port. People are offloaded in the early morning hours, and buses are on the road before most people are up."

"One innovation he came up with was to have the cargo sorted into groups on the ship based on destination. Forty people in each group. The bus for Atlanta pulls up, that group disembarks, gets on the bus, and the bus leaves. The bus for Washington DC is right behind, and that group disembarks, and so on. We can have all the buses loaded and out of the dock area in less than a half hour."

"I'm surprised they know where they want to go," I say.

"About two-thirds do. We fill in the remaining numbers for that bus by putting the next undecided person in that group," Tony says with a smile. "Poor souls don't know where they're going."

"Gustaf tells me the New York Don is considering starting a new operation in Boston. This might be a little much, possibly attracting DHS's attention."

"George, I learned a long time ago not to question the Don. I share your concerns, but questioning the Don poses greater risks than DHS. At least with DHS, I remain alive."

***

Several days later I got a panic call from Tony. "The Coast Guard has just boarded the Fada do Carro. They're taking it to Charleston to impound it. There are over four hundred illegals on it. We're screwed!"

This is not good. "Tony, take a deep breath. I'll be there in ten minutes."

Tony's warehouse is in a state of meltdown when I get there. The Bulk is burning records. Other minions are loading incriminating evidence into bins to be taken – taken somewhere where the feds won't find it.

I find Tony in his office. He's on the phone talking to his New York cousins. It looks like the Miami mob is getting ready to pull up stakes. Tony, "Let's talk," I say over the din. He looks up as I ask, "Can they tie the ship to you? I thought Coastal Shipping was the owner?"

"They are."

"You don't have any formal lease or contract with them do you? Any paper trail?" I ask.

"No."

"Do you think the Captain will flip on the mob?"

81

"Not if he values his family," Tony says.

"Okay," I say, "maybe we can ride this out. Can you contact the Captain before they arrive at Charleston?"

Tony thinks for a minute, "He has a burner phone for emergencies like this."

"Okay, contact him and have him tell the first mate and other crew members he has concerns about to keep their mouths shut. Tell him you will take care of them and their families."

"Now, where are Stan and his drivers?" I ask.

"They're at Jacksonville, waiting for the ship to dock."

Call him and tell him to get the buses out of there, disperse them. And you want to see him later today, here. He needs to quietly close down his network."

"I think we can contain this. The feds will be here, probably in the morning. Our story, we don't know anything. I'll line Michael up to represent whoever is caught up in this, but we need to keep Michael mostly in the dark."

20: Busted

Tuesday morning, early August, there are two feds in the building looking for me. They scare the crap out of Angelic. Michael sends them to my office on the third floor. Jeromy tries to run interference in the outer office, but sheer muscle mass wins. They are in my office, Jeromy still fighting a rearguard action.

"Are you George Basdakis?" the smaller of the two asks.

"And you are?"

He pulls out his shield wallet, flips it open, "I'm FBI Agent Oscar Baker. You need to come with us."

"I don't think so!"

Oscar pulls out a warrant for my arrest. The big agent slaps cuffs on me. As they hustle me out of the office, I yell to Jeromy, "Get Michael to wherever these goons are taking me! Probably the federal courthouse!"

The detention center is in the federal courthouse. I'm in an integration room in the basement for fifteen or twenty minutes when a new player enters.

"Mr. Basdakis, I'm Agent Dillion with the FBI. Your name has come up in our investigation of a mob smuggling operation. We want to talk with you."

"Let's wait for my attorney," I say.

"We could, but the deal I'm going to offer you, well, perhaps you would like to keep it quiet." Without further ado, he pulls out his cell phone and plays a few taped recordings of phone calls between Tony and me. Next, he plays a video. It's Juan Reyes. He's laying out the complete Coastal Shipping operation. He names me as the originator of the people moving venture. He even provides a clip from his phone showing me addressing the Coastal Shipping Board.

"Juan is the nail in the coffin for you," says Dillard. "He's a Brazilian Federal Police undercover agent. To use a law enforcement term, 'your goose is cooked.'"

About then Michael enters the room. "Stop!" he shouts. "George, don't say another word."

I look up at Michael and say, "I think there's been a misunderstanding. Agent Dillard and I are having a private discussion. I'll call you later."

He looks at me with some disbelief and walks out.

Looking at Dillard, "Okay, what's the deal."

"You turn states evidence. We want Tony. We want the New York mob. Brazil wants Coastal Shipping. Nobody wants you," Dillard says.

"You know if I do this, I'm on everyone's hit list. What's the chance of getting into the witness protection program?" I ask.

"Well, it's possible, but that's above my pay grade. In the morning we'll visit the Miami Federal Prosecutor's office to see what they will agree to. But for the night you are our guest," Dillard says with a smirk.

The prosecutor's office buys off on the deal. They hold me for two more days while they make videos of my confession, of me hanging Tony out to dry, and of what little I know about his New York cousins. Regrettably, I'm forced to rat on the Scorpion gang. I really did want to keep Stan out of this.

On the second day, Juan shows up and has me dump the dirt on Gustaf and Coastal Shipping.

At the end of the second day, Dillion has me fitted with an ankle monitor and tells me I'm free – as long as I stay in the city.

Later at my office, Jeromy's first question is, "What happened?" I give him a thumbnail sketch.

"You know your dead, don't you?" Jeromy says.

"Ya," I say, thinking there is no promotion at the end of this episode.

That night I made a phone call to my uncle, Uncle Christos. He's my father's brother, the black sheep of the family. He and I have always gotten along well. His son Nicholas and I were like peas in a pod growing up, often mistaken as twins.

Christos and I concoct a plan. The next day I convinced Jeromy to lend me his car. Maybe lend is not the right word. In about six hours, he will report it stolen. By then, I'll be in the Florida Panhandle, and it will be dark. Uncle Christos will have one of his people meet me in Pensacola, where I'll abandon Jeromy's car. Dillard's ankle bracelet is left in my bottom desk drawer.

Later that night, Christos is waiting for me. Now Christos is an interesting guy. He works a bit on the shady side of the law. He runs a Greek import/export business. As a young man, he worked for a Greek antique dealer in Biloxi. Many claimed he dealt with stolen artifacts. Seeing a huge profit margin, Christos started a similar import/export business in Mobile. Over the years, he expanded the business, leasing an old freighter with Greek registration.

His son Nicholas was reported missing in Afghanistan a few years ago. As far as the feds are concerned, Nicholas is neither here nor there – he's missing. Christos holds the government responsible and has no qualms about working outside the law. He has given up hope of seeing Nicholas again. I tell him my story. After some thought, he asked if I wanted to work for him in Greece.

Well, what choice do I have? This is a new opportunity. He gives me his son's passport, which won't expire for several more years. Three days later Nicholas Basdakis is signed on to Christos's freighter as a junior officer. My Navy experience is a help; I know the bow from the stern, but not much more. I'm bound for Corfu.

21: Corfu

Corfu is on a small island off the West Coast of Greece. Corfu's claim to fame is it's the birthplace of Prince Philip, the consort to Queen Elizabeth. It's a quiet city with a quiet port, an ideal transshipment point for questionable cargo.

My role? As mentioned above, Christos got his start in the trade with a Greek dealer in antiquities. As Christos aged, he became more enamored with Greek artifacts. My college degree is in European history, with a minor in archaeology. At least I knew the difference between Mesolithic and Neolithic. I was to work with Christos's contact, Kyriakos Mitsotakis, an elderly gentleman on the verge of retirement, with the idea I'd take over the operation. My role, select artifacts to be smuggled to Christos. Christos would then sell them to museums, collectors and possibly keep one or two for himself.

My first stop was the city's Registry Office, where I applied for Greek citizenship. Under Greek law, children of Greek parents were Greek. My parents were both Greek, immigrating to America in the 1970s. I qualified. George Basdakis was reborn. I was not worried about extradition. The Greek government frowned upon the extradition of Greek citizens for mundane crimes like smuggling. With citizenship came access to a Greek passport.

Next, a quick flight to Cyprus. I needed to transfer assets from my numbered account in the Caribbean to a new account before the FBI located my booty. It took the Central Bank of Cyprus less than an hour to open an account and transfer assets, $5.2 million, from my old account. The bank manager assured me that the transfer could not be traced. Before leaving the bank, I directed a half million be transferred to a new account I had established in Corfu with the Bank of Greece. Pocket money.

Back in Corfu, Kyriakos Mitsotakis makes it a practice to visit new archaeological sites; he wants first crack at pilfered artifacts. He recently learned of a new site in the mountains not far from Pyrgos, a small village dating back to the Bronze Age.

"Nicholas, or is it George? I get confused," said Kyriakos. We're going to Pyrgos in the morning.

"Okay, great," now I'm playing Indiana Jones, I'm thinking.

Early the following day, we set sail, figuratively. Kyriakos has an old diesel-powered yacht he refitted to serve as his 'retrieval vessel,' as he liked to call it. Pyrgos is a coastal town on the west side of the Peloponnese peninsula.

As we pulled out of the harbor, Kyriakos says, "Christos tells me you are a navy man; you take the bridge while I take a nap,"

The yacht's Captain, a middle-aged man named Adrian, is standing nearby. "Okay, where to boss," he says with mirth.

"I have no f-----g idea! You got the keys to this f-----g boat; you figure it out," I snap.

"Yes sir, boss," Adrian replies with a laugh.

"Pyrgos is about ten hours south. If you are inclined, pull up a seat. I'll give you some navigation lessons for sailing in Greek waters. There're some treacherous stretches along the coast, some vicious currents." The next several hours were educational.

22: Pyrgos

We arrive at a marina not far from Pyrgos, well before sunset. Kyriakos has a rental car waiting. As we load our bags into the trunk, Kyriakos flips me the keys, saying, "You drive George. Pyrgos is ten kilometers up the road. Stay on the road; you can't miss our hotel, The Misty Isles." He slips into the backseat and shuts his eyes.

The road follows the coast, the ocean on one side and olive trees on the other. The countryside appears sparsely populated. The hillsides have mostly olive groves. I see a hint of a forest in the ravines between the hills. Pyrgos is a couple kilometers inland, a dusty town with few storefronts. I find The Misty Isles Hotel on the far side of town. Given the number of Range Rovers in the parking lot, I'm guessing the archaeologists, those excavating the new discovery, are staying here. "Of course they are; why else would Kyriakos bring me here."

As we enter the hotel's lobby, a shifty old man dressed as an explorer from the 1920s approaches. "Kyriakos, it's good to see you again. Didn't know if you'd be here or not. Heard rumors of your retirement, you know. I see you've employed a driver."

"Archie, you old dog. You haven't drained the bar, have you? A stiff drink is needed after such an arduous journey. But first, let me introduce you to George Basdakis. He's my understudy, who will be taking over the business one of these days." And as they drift toward the bar and his voice fades, "Any good finds..."

I find the reception desk. Kyriakos has reserved two rooms on the upper floor. The hotel's boy helps with the bags. I have Kyriakos's gear placed in the larger room, the room facing the street. I take the smaller and hopefully quieter room.

Returning downstairs, I find Kyriakos and Archie at a table, with full glasses, reminiscing about old digs. Walking up to the table "Kyriakos, I saw a small restaurant as we drove in. Are you interested in getting something to eat?"

"No, I'll get a sandwich from the bar. Enjoy yourself."

"You're in Room 5, 'The Adonis Suite,' on the third floor. Here's the key."

"George, if I don't see you again tonight, we plan to meet up with the dig team at nine in the morning. See you here in the lobby."

As I turn to leave, a young lady in jeans and a bush jacket comes up behind Archie, "Archie, skipping dinner again?"

He brushes her off, saying, "Karen, why don't you join Kyriakos's apprentice here? Jerry, wasn't it? He's going to that rat trap they call a restaurant."

I look at her, nod toward the door, and we both walk out.

The restaurant is a cut above a rat trap; it's adequate. Leaving the hotel, I reintroduce myself. "My name is George, not Jerry, and I'm not Kyriakos's apprentice. Did I hear Archie call you Karen?"

The restaurant has a nice menu. We order the house special and a local bottle of wine. We talked a bit. I give her a redacted version of myself. "I'm a historian with a working knowledge of archeology. My uncle, Christof Basdakis, wants me to take over Kyriakos's operation when he retires, which is expected soon. This is my first taste of fieldwork. And what is your background?"

"Well, as you know, my name is Karen, Karen Wilson. I'm a postgraduate student at the University of Manchester, where Dr. Brown, Archie, is a professor. This is my second dig with him, probably the last. Last summer, we worked on a small site in Turkey with only moderate success. Speaking out of school, he's more successful excavating whiskey bottles than artifacts."

"Ouch, that's harsh," I say.

"But true!"

23: The Dig

The next morning I'm enjoying the hotel's continental breakfast but wishing for traditional English fare when other members of our group fill the other table; Dr. Brown has two postgraduate students at his table, Karren and Thomas. Kyriakos, returning from the breakfast bar with a coffee refill, says to Archie, "I didn't expect to see you up so early."

Not missing a beat Archie, with blurry and red-ringed eyes, responds, "Wouldn't miss this morning." I see Karen roll her eyes.

Leaving the hotel, Kyriakos and I are following the two Range Rovers Karen and Thomas are driving.

Getting into our rental, Kyriakos starts, "Archie drinks like a fish. Thought I'd never get to bed. It would help if you stayed on his good side; he's one of our sources, one of our better sources of illicit finds. He will sell us pieces on the side that his team digs up. He needs money to pay bar tabs. There is no need to mention this to Karren or Thomas."

Kyriakos goes on with a short history lesson. "This dig is supposedly a village abandoned over three thousand years ago. A relic of the Mycenaean civilization. If properly dated, it may have been sacked by the Sea People. About 1200 BC, the eastern Mediterranean was invaded by seaborn warriors from the western Mediterranean; some think they originated in Sicily. This invasion spanned several hundred years and contributed to the collapse of the Mycenaean, Hittite, and Babylon empires. Egypt also took some heavy hits."

"How is a site like this hidden for thousands of years?" I ask.

"It wasn't hidden, just not noticed," Kyriakos says. "After the collapse of the Mycenaean civilization, Greece entered a period called 'The Greek Dark Ages' which lasted several hundred years. Until the Middle Ages, this area was sparsely populated due to wars, earthquakes, and volcanic eruptions. Over time the village's skeleton was partially covered. The few inhabitants gave the outcroppings of ancient walls little thought; they just planted around them. There are sites like this all over Greece. And, for that matter, Turkey and the Levant."

We arrive at the site located a dozen or so kilometers south of Pyrgos. It sits on a hillside overlooking the Ionian Sea. The team's earlier work, utilizing local labor, has uncovered several building foundations. One can see remnants of the ancient road that meandered through the village.

As Karren and Thomas tackle one area with their trowels and brushes, I ask Karren, "What do you hope to find?"

"We think this is or was a kitchen. Pottery shards, utensils, bones, or such not, may help date this site. Yesterday, along the outer wall, we found several bronze arrowheads consistent with the middle bronze period. The people who lived here were farmers.

95

The arrowheads were the type the sea invaders used. That, along with the charred remains we found, suggests the village was attacked."

I'm sitting on one of the outer walls looking down at the sea. I'm wondering what happened here, what people's lives were like in this village when it was sacked.

1231 BC

Lena is sitting on a bench next to the wall nursing her newborn daughter. Her two boys, two and three years old, are playing at her feet. She's looking down at where her husband and his two brothers are plowing the land for spring planting. Her husband is guiding the plow, the two brothers pulling it. Looking up at the sea, she sees sails, many sails coming over the horizon.

Yelling out for her sister-in-law, "Helen, quick, come out here!"

"I'm fixing lunch for the men; I'll be there in a minute."

"NOW!"

As Helen comes out the door, Lena points to the sea. As the sight registers in Helen's mind, she drops the dish she's carrying and runs down the hill to where the men are. She's wildly waving her arms. The men drop the plow, and the four race back to the village, sounding the alarm.

Women come out wondering what's going on. They're told to grab what they can and take the children to the caves in the next valley. Lena's sister-in-law, the eldest of the group, leads them up the hill into the woods. There are sixteen women, twenty-seven children, the oldest are helping the youngest. From here, it's normally an hour's hike. With the kids, it will be much longer today.

Hearing the alarm brings other menfolk from their daily chores to see what the commotion is. They quickly form into groups herding the livestock up the hill into the woods. Some collect items that can serve as weapons, a few bronze axes, knives, and farm implements. They abandon the village, but the livestock is critical to the village's survival. They form a defensive line hidden on the edge of the forest. Perhaps, if they are lucky, the marauders will overlook them.

Two days later, Lena's youngest brother-in-law staggers into the cave. He's badly wounded. He tells the women, "There are only two or three survivors who were able to flee into the woods" he says. "Leana, your husband is dead. He led the charge into the marauder's ranks wielding his axe."

Over the next few days, people drift back to the village, or what was the village. Everything has been burned to the ground. Two other men who managed to escape are badly wounded. Food stores have been looted. The spring planting seed is gone. Some of the livestock is rounded up, carcasses of others are found in the woods, and the rest have wandered off.

Helen is now the leader. The three surviving men, each seriously injured, concede leadership to her. It is decided the villagers should go inland.

Later that day, Kyriakos pulls me aside. In the back of our rental, he has a wrapped package. "Open that up George and tell me what you think."

I do as he asks. I find some broken pottery, perhaps enough for a whole vase. "And this is?" I ask.

"I just purchased that from Archie for an unbelievably small amount. His team uncovered it yesterday. An excellent example of Mycenaean pottery."

In my hands, I'm holding a piece of pottery depicting classical Greek warriors.

"Kyriakos, I hope it was a very small amount. At best, this is from the Hellenistic period. I expect to find a Pottery Barn label on one of the missing fragments. You know as well as I do the Trojan war motifs didn't occur on pottery until well after Homer's death. This artwork reflects adventures from the *Iliad*, Homer's epic poem. He died in the 7th century BC. At best, this is no older than the 5th century BC."

"Well done," says Kyriakos.

24: Vrettos Antiques

It's been four years since my encounter with Dillion. I've built a comfortable life in Corfu. Two years ago, I bought a small villa on a hillside on the outskirts of town. The villa overlooks the town. On a clear day, I can see the mainland. I've had a few romantic encounters, but mostly the local women have one thing on their minds ... marriage.

Karen returned with Archie the summer after we first met. I could have tied the knot with her, except she was engaged to some entitled lord's son, a twit as Archie described him. Last year Archie told me she was married and expecting.

Kyriakos and I visited many digs during three of these years. He introduced me to the less scrupulous archaeologists. He developed relationships with several antiquity dealers over the years. I was introduced to them as his protégé. They all shared Kyriakos's moral compass. In short, he was turning over his illicit empire to me.

Last year Kyriakos sold me his shop and yacht for a substantial price and retired. He was returning to Kavala, the city of his birth. Kavala is on the other side of Greece, at the north end of the Aegean Sea, a good location for Mycenaean artifacts, he claimed. He was going to open a small curio shop as a hobby to fleece the occasional tourist. He promised to keep me in mind if he came across any good finds.

For the past several years, Kyriakos and I have kept Christos happy. Three or four times a year his freighter would make a port call at Corfu. We would load the ship's 'hidden hold' with the antiques being smuggled out of the country. It wasn't so much that the hold was hidden, the illicit storage area was buried beneath, and behind the legitimate cargo, cargoes made up of dried fish, pharmaceuticals, electronics, nuts, dried fruits, etc.

Christos ran a very profitable import-export business. I always wondered why he jeopardized it by smuggling antiques. I know he was enamored with Greek artifacts, some of which he sold for a modest profit. But overall, it was a risky business with small payback. I know. I sunk a well-functioning hot car export enterprise by expanding into people moving. The latter caught the fed's attention, bringing down the whole international enterprise.

On Kyriakos's last day, Christos calls the shop to wish him well.

"Kyriakos, I am going to miss you. We've been working together for what, the past two decades? I lose track of time. I'll miss you."

"It won't be a big loss," Kyriakos responds. "George is ready to take over. He's been running the business for the past year or so."

"George," Christos says, "setting family aside, you've been one of my better investments. I'm looking forward to our future,"

"Kyriakos has been a good mentor, introducing me to his contacts and selling me his shop. I'm headed to Athens next week, where we, I guess it's just me now, have a new source of possible merchandise. As you know, antique dealers here are notorious thieves. Kyriakos has been invaluable in helping me weed them out. Let's see how I do solo."

"I'm sure you will do fine. I'm looking forward to seeing what you find. To set your mind at ease, I plan to up my payments to you by 10 percent, which should help reimburse your recent expenses.

***

Three weeks later, I'm standing with the Captain on the bridge as he edges the yacht into its assigned slip. We are using one of the small marinas on the city's east side.

"Adrian, why this marina?" I ask.

"It's used mostly by locals; the police tend to leave it alone. And, the marina is managed by my brother-in-law; he has our back."

"I suggest the Urban Suites as a place to stay; rooms are modestly priced," he continues. "It was one of Kyriakos's favorites. Mention his name, you might get a discount."

Adrian is right; Urban Suites is an excellent choice. I get a suite on an upper floor with a nice harbor view. Kyriakos's name gets me VIP treatment.

That afternoon Adrian and I visited a small antique shop, the *Vrettos Antiques*. Over the past year, I have involved Adrian in more of my business dealings. Not knowledgeable about antiques; he's an expert on people. He can flag a bullshitter from fifty paces.

Vrettos Antiques is a small shop not far from the Acropolis. One can stand in the store's vestibule, see the Parthenon, the temple to the Greek goddess Athena, and be inclined to part with their euros as an offering to the city.

A young lady, busy dusting the bric-a-brac, looks up and greets us. She does a double-take when she sees me.

"Welcome to *Vrettos Antiques*; how can I help you? We have many marvelous items. What can I show you?"

Adrian's BS detector is flashing as he says, "Sorry to bother you. We took a wrong turn back there; thought this was the flea market."

"Actually, we are here to see Mr. Pappas. I believe he is the owner of this fine establishment," I say, hoping to placate the ire Adrian's comment caused.

Somewhat mollified, "I'll get him; he's in the back."

She quickly returns with a small man in tow. He's an elderly gentleman, neither tall nor short, wearing bifocal glasses.

"My daughter says you are asking for me," Mr. Pappas says, "how can I help?"

"My former colleague, Kyriakos Mitsotakis, now retired, gave me your name. He suggested we might be able to do business."

"Ah, Kyriakos" the old man says. "It's been years since I've seen him. Five or six years ago, I sold him several pieces of what I thought was Mycenaean pottery. The pieces turned out to be reproductions. He accused me of fraud. Our relationship was rather frosty for the next few years."

"That's the story Kyriakos told me," I say. "But, apparently other dealers hold you in high esteem, and Kyriakos thought he may have been a little hasty. Before retiring, he suggested I call on you at some point, noting that you had always been a reliable partner prior to the misunderstanding."

"George, is it? Please call me Alexis. Let's go into the backroom where it's more comfortable. Elena, get us some tea and biscuits."

Alexis has a small 'man cave' in the back. A couch, two overstuffed chairs, and a medium size flatscreen TV. A still burning pipe was on a side table next to one of the chairs, and a soccer game was playing on the muted TV.

"That's a rerun of yesterday's match between AEK Athens and the Panathinaikos. Don't tell me the outcome; I missed the game yesterday."

"Actually, I don't know."

After the next score, Alexis turned the set off; his team was losing – badly.

"I'm hoping you might have some old pottery lying around that I can take off your hands ... at a reasonable price."

"I don't have anything that would interest you at the moment. But, my son-in-law, Elena's husband, will be offloading some items he recently obtained in Crete from a German archaeological dig. He needs to wait until his police buddy is on duty."

"Can you come back in the morning, about ten?" Alexis asks.

25: Nicholas

The following morning Adrian and I returned to Vrettos Antiques. It's my turn to do a double-take. There behind the counter is Nicholas.

"Nicholas! I thought you were dead."

He looks up and, with a big smile, comes around the counter and gives me a big hug. George, it's good to see you. "When my father-in-law mentioned your name last night, I was convinced it must be a different George Basdakis. Let's go in the back and we can talk."

We spent the rest of the morning telling our tales. He was dumbstruck when I mentioned I was working for his father, impressed with my people moving scheme. He noted something on that scale would spring leaks, which it did, and said he had heard of Fat Leonard.

His story was a bit more somber.

"As you know, I enlisted in the army after high school. Did my basic and advanced infantry training, AIT, at Fort Polk. After Ft. Polk, I was assigned to the 3rd Brigade, 4th Infantry Division. I did two tours in Iraq, where I was involved in some heavy fighting. My third tour went downhill. In 2012 my platoon was assigned to liaison with the Yazidis who had taken refuge from ISIS on Mount Sinjar,

"Unbeknownst to us, the 3rd Brigade pulled back to Bagdad, leaving my platoon stranded. After a week of heavy fighting, only four of us were left, and with very little ammunition. The Kurds came to our rescue and evacuated the Yazidis and the four of us behind their lines, northeast of Kirkuk.

"We joined the Kurds in fending off the troglodytes. We lost two more men. It was then, several months from our initial deployment, and what did I hear on the BBC? American forces have been reduced to a bare minimum; the 4th Infantry Division has been pulled out of the country. We were on our own.

"Corporal Davis and I, over some local brew, spent one long night deciding what to do. He liked it there. A local prosecutor was waiting for him back in New York. The leader's daughter caught his eye. At the daughter's urging, Davis talked to her father, Mahmud Zadeh, and they were married.

"Since I could qualify for Greek citizenship, I traveled from Kurdistan, thru Turkey, to Greece. Once here, I got a job with Mr. Pappas. From there, the rest is obvious. I met Elena, we got married. I took her last name, so my papers identify me as Nicholas Pappas."

"That's quite a story," I say. "Have you contacted your father?"

106

"No, and I don't want you to mention me to him. It would destroy him if he knew I was a deserter."

"You were the one abandoned!"

"That's beside the point," he says. I'll be painted as a deserter, and he will see that as discrediting him. Please don't say anything to him. Nicholas Basdakis is dead."

26: Magdalen

Over the next several months, more like a year, Nicholas and I combined our efforts to pilfer Greek artifacts. He sold mostly to two or three Asian buyers, buyers who were interested in Hellenistic pottery. I channeled my finds through Christos, who wanted Mycenaean artifacts. We bought from farmers who unearthed treasures when plowing their fields, from illicit dealers who, more often than not, were selling reproductions, and on the sly from state-sponsored archaeological digs such as that of Dr. Brown of the University of Manchester.

I've been spending a week or so every month in Athens. As with most married ladies, Elena is always looking to find me a mate. Why is it wives can't resist playing matchmakers? The three of us, Elena, Nicholas, and I, were attending a social outing honoring the city's antique dealers. As we arrive at the banquet hall, Elena takes my arm, leads me across the room, and introduces me to Magdalen.

"Magdalen, this is George, the one I was telling you about."

"George, this is Magdalen, an old friend; we went to school together. I thought you two might like to meet. You have much in common," she says as she wanders off.

Great, I'm thinking this is the third time Elena has introduced me to an 'old friend.' She's set me up for another boring night.

Magdalen, although not eye candy, is not unattractive. She's a few inches shorter than me, with brunette hair and olive-brown eyes. I'd guess her age is late twenties.

She looks me in the eye and says, "You look disappointed. I take it this is not the first time Elena has blindsided you. I'm here for my father. He dabbles in the trade. I understand you smuggle antiques." She is now reminding me of a young Helen back in Miami.

I am somewhat speechless. Here is an attractive young lady, apparently soliciting illicit business for her father. I'm intrigued. I grab two flutes of champagne from a passing waiter and suggest we move to one of the tables to talk.

"Magdalen, that's a lovely name. Apparently, Elena has dumped the goods on me; tell me about yourself."

"My father owns three-night clubs ... and dabbles as a fence for fine jewelry. I'm his understudy. See that large man by the palm tree; he's my bodyguard. What else would you like to know?"

My interest is peaked. Elena did good this time. Over the coming months, I spend a fair amount of time with Magdalen. She introduces me to her father, Demetri, who, at our first meeting, is asking about moving stolen cars. Who in Athens doesn't know my history, I'm wondering.

I spend some time describing Tony's operation. I go into detail recounting my conception of and implementing the 'people

109

moving' program. I gloss over the operation's demise, and my turning states evidence; didn't seem relevant to our conversation. When he asks if I'd be interested in working for him in a similar endeavor, I decline, explaining my small antique smuggling enterprise keeps me busy. But I thank him for the offer.

On our outings, Magdalen is always accompanied by her bodyguard. "Ignore him," she tells me. "Ever since an attempted abduction three years ago by one of my father's rivals, my father is insistent he is with me."

Okay, a little muscle never hurt. I make it a practice to buy Calix, a Greek name meaning 'hansom' which he does not reflect, a coffee or dinner depending on where we are. He won't touch alcohol; Demetri would have his nuts if he did.

Magdalen is taking me to the Parthenon on one of our sightseeing outings. As we blend into a group of tourists, I'm hit in the back of my head and fall headfirst onto the pavement. As a crowd gathers around, I see Magdalen's bodyguard has a body pinned to the ground and is preparing to beat on it with his massive fists.

I tell Calix to hold off; he's sitting on top of Gustaf! Now, this is an interesting development.

"Gustaf, what the hell are you doing in Athens?"

As Gustaf gets up, he starts to tell me his story while eyeing Calix.

"We've created enough of a scene here," I say, "there is a quiet café at the base of the Acropolis where we can talk."

It turns out Gustaf was one step ahead of the police when Coastal Shipping was raided. Using fake documents, he fled Brazil and has been plying the Mediterranean as a carefree retired entrepreneur ever since.

After I tell my tale of being set up by <u>his</u> hand-picked person, Juan Reyes, an undercover police agent, Gustaf has nothing to say. Apparently, he didn't know he was harboring a state viper. Brazilian authorities never revealed Reyes's role, keeping him unnamed in the proceedings, ready for future stings. Gustaf becomes a little more forgiving as he learns about Juan.

"Gustaf, to show there are no hard feelings, let me introduce you to Magdalen's father, Demetri. He is interested in moving stolen cars to North Africa and looking for someone with experience to head up the operation."

27: The Business Lady

Demetri and Gustaf hit it off from the start. Demetri greased the skids, so to speak, in helping Gustaf get a residency permit. Gustaf then helps organize and manage Demetri's new smuggling operation.

Demetri's business associates have access to several old, Greek-flagged freighters that moved cargo between Mediterranean ports and Europe's Atlantic Seaboard. The operation that emerged was rather elegant I have to admit. Late model stolen vehicles, cars, SUVs, vans, etc., were loaded as freight onto a ship at any of several European ports. But no more than four of five per trip. The vehicles were offloaded at a North African port a few days later. With the several ships, the operation moved a hundred cars a year – providing a handsome profit for the investors with minimum risk.

Occasionally I found myself kicking myself for not taking Demetri up on his initial offer – until Interpol descended on one of the ships being loaded in Marseille. Unlike the Greek authorities, Interpol was hardnose when it came to smuggling.

Demetri was able to avoid arrest by claiming ignorance; he did not know what Gustaf was doing, and he did not know Gustaf's history. Demetri's business associates lost their investments; the freighters initially impounded, but with a bit of behind-the-scenes wheedling, were eventually returned to the associates who went on with their other illicit endeavors. Gustaf, again one step ahead of the authorities, found himself plying Southeast Asia as a carefree retired entrepreneur.

***

As I said, Magdalen and I were becoming an item. We watched the rise and fall of her father's hot car venture from the sidelines, staying well away from it. Over coffee one day, I'm not sure who suggested it, but we agreed we should try living together. She would join me in Corfu.

Magdalen had visited my home for an occasional weekend, but now it was full-time. There was only so much a girl from the big city could do in Corfu without going stir-crazy. She suggested working in my import-export business. *'The Basdakis Shipping Brokerage Co.'*, BSB Co., had become a viable enterprise, with Christos's business playing a shrinking role each year.

I'd buy Greek olives and sell them in London. Working with French pharmaceutical companies, I'd find Greek suppliers – and make sure I had the shipping contract. I successfully dabbled in this and that.

A few years earlier I purchased a dockside warehouse which I used as a transshipment hub. Magdalen took over the management of the warehouse, managing the inventory and shipping schedules.

Magdalen excelled in this role. She was soon involved in negotiating deals, matching new buyers with sellers, and in general, managing the operation. Now Magdalen was no timid wallflower and was soon pressing for a larger role – partnership.

Now how did I get into this position? My feelings for the girl were strong and getting stronger. I trusted her. But the deciding factor was comments reflected by a few of my newer and more established customers, "Magdalen is the reason I'm doing business with BSB Co." they said. "I trust her." Over wine on the patio one evening we agreed to a 30/70 partnership split, Magdalen thirty me seventy, which would be renegotiated in a year.

By this time Christos was nearing retirement. His appetite for Greek artifacts was waning. This was good. Magdalen was insistent that all aspects of BSB Co. be above board. Christos and I had an amenable parting of the way with regard to smuggling, but we remained his prime contact for legal cargo. Magdalen's trip to Mobile charmed the pants off him, figuratively.

28: The Past

Things were great. The business was booming, I see Nicolas every couple of months, and he and I still manage an 'archaeology recovery' expedition two or three times a year. Magdalen and I have a little George running around. Nicholas and Elena doted on him.

With little George's arrival, Magdalen has become Maggi. We have both skirted the 'marriage' topic. She is reluctant to lose her independence, at least as she sees it in the Greek culture, and I'm clinging to youth as represented by my bachelorhood. Although we have not set a date, we both know it's coming.

Things were going good, too good. That's when an elderly gentleman, Mr. Markopoulos, arrived at my doorstep late one afternoon.

"I am a senior minister with the Ministry of Commerce and find myself involved in a significant problem affecting the country's economic well-being. As you know, shipping is one of Greece's significant money-makers. Due to rampant corruption and bribery, the industry is suffering. We at the Ministry of Commerce need to take corrective actions. To do that, we need inside information. If I can come in, I have something to discuss with you."

With an offer like that, what could I say? I invited him out to the patio which was secluded and quiet. "Coffee or tea, I asked?" He declines.

"Mr. Basdakis, first, I would like to talk with you about your past misdeeds," he said. "During the affair with Gustaf's smuggling exploits, your name, more specifically your picture, came to my attention," he said.

"But before I get to the topic that brought me here today, I need to talk about the past. It's a story of deceit and betrayal," starts Markopoulos. "I was an associate of your father. I participated in Papadopoulos's military junta which took control of the country in the '60s. Your father and two brothers were with us, or so we thought. They were responsible for the death of my parents when they sold us out."

My family history, recounted by Christos, was flashing through my mind. My father and uncle were part of the movement to undermine Papandreou's dictatorship in the '60s. Due to unfortunate actions by my father and uncle, specifically firebombing a political opponent's home, my family was forced to flee Greece. There was an older brother named Alexander, but I knew nothing of him.

Continuing his story, Markopoulos says, "My sons took it upon themselves to satisfy the family's vendetta against those who killed their grandparents. I tried to convince them to drop it; those were events from another time. It was like talking to the deaf. As you know, fishing boats were blown-up, killing your father and uncle. For that, I am sorry. My sons are now serving multiple life sentences in one of your prisons."

"I saw your picture in the paper, a spitting image of your father. I did a little research and, with more than a little effort, unearthed your colorful past. A past demonstrating skills we need. We were most impressed with your people-moving enterprise. I'm also aware of your smuggling of artifacts. Christos, your 'good' uncle, and I were, and still are, friends. His desire for artifacts was always at a personal level, and that more than offset the business he brought to the country. For him, we turned a blind eye; for you …"

"I'm not sure I like where this is going," I say. "What's in it for me?"

"Not much really. Mabey we can defer a pending tax audit that we've scheduled for next year."

"And how am I to help you?" I ask.

"Shipping is the backbone of the Greek economy. In recent years growing graft and kickbacks have threatened the Greek shipping industry. We want your company, BSB Co., to join the Greek Shipping Guild and become our inside eyes and ears."

"You want me to become a snitch?"

"We would rather phrase it as being an informant."

"I need to discuss this with my partner. I'll call you."

29: The Guild

At first, Maggi was reluctant to have any part of Markopoulos's proposal. She complained to **Demetri,** her father, that I was trying to turn the company into a police informant. Now Demetri, through his nightclubs, has hidden interests in several enterprises, many that even Magdalen is unaware of, one being *Parrhasius Shipping.*

"Magdalen joining the Guild might not be a bad idea. You could help the family business with inside information," Demetri told his daughter.

Two days later I called Markopoulos. "I'm in, but one condition, Magdalen will be BSB Co's representative. She is the one who is expanding the company's footprint and the one most exporters now deal with. I'm just the shmuck holding the company's mortgage."

"That will be a problem; the Shipping Guild is composed of elite males."

"Well, apply some pressure, bring them into the 21st century. Maggi will give them a fresh perspective. Mabey the threat of a tax audit, will get their attention," I say tongue-in-cheek.

A week later, **Maggi** gets a call from the secretary of the Greek Shipping Guild asking if she would be available to meet with the Guild's president the following Monday. An appointment is made, and by the end of the month, Magdalen is a seated member of the Guild.

***

Maggi continues to expand BSB Co. In August, she dispatched me to Rotterdam to meet a new client, a novelty toy manufacturer looking for a shipper to import subassemblies from Greece.

I have a ten a.m. meeting scheduled with Herr Gerhardt. Boehringer Ltd.'s corporate office occupies the top three floors of one of the more prominent office buildings that make up Rotterdam's skyline. I pass through the building's security checkpoint. As I get into the express elevator, I'm joined by a rather small and obnoxious man. With a guttural Dutch accent, he introduces himself. "I'm Peter Gerhardt, Herr Gerhardt's nephew. And you are George Basdakis. We've been expecting you."

Now I'm a good judge of character, and Peter Gerhardt is a sleazeball. He exits to the left when the elevator doors open.

I find myself in Boehringer Ltd.'s outer office lobby. Herr Gerhardt's secretary ushers me into his private meeting room and offers me coffee telling me they will be in shortly. A few minutes later, the door at the other end of the room opens, and several men come in and take seats around the table. An older man comes up to me and introduces himself as Earnest Gerhardt.

"Mr. Basdakis, thank you for meeting with us. As you know, we are looking for a shipping company to move parts for our toys from Greece to our factories here in Holland. BSB Co. is highly recommended as a shipping broker ....." And so the meeting went on for the next half hour. By the end of the meeting, I had a signed contract giving BSB Co. exclusive rights to serve as Boehringer Ltd.'s shipping agent for the next twelve months.

As I'm putting the contract in my briefcase, who waltzes in? Peter.

"George," Earnest starts; we are on first name bases by now, "I'd like to introduce you to my nephew, Peter. Peter represents some shipping firms in Greece. Perhaps you two should talk."

On the elevator ride down, my BS antenna is fully engaged as Peter hands me a business card for one of his clients, Parrhasius Shipping. "I think we are on the same flight tomorrow going to Athens. Let's meet in your hotel lobby before the flight, and we can discuss specifics," Peter says with a grin.

To make a long story short, we meet for breakfast. When he went to the restroom, I rummaged through his carry-on, found his airline ticket, and copied key information from it. Later under the pretext of using the men's room, I used a hotel phone and called the airline agent that issued Peter's ticket. I reported that the ticket was missing, probably stolen this morning. At the airport, after we boarded, two police officers, along with the airline representative, escorted Peter off the plane. As I later learned, he was arrested for using a stolen ticket.

30: Demetri

Since I was returning to Athens, Maggi decided to meet at the airport and has a quiet weekend, away from little George and day-to-day business pressures planned for us. Nicholas and Elena are taking us to a new restaurant they found that serves only traditional Greek food, no fusion cuisine.

We are happily seated in the main dining area. The first course, Penne Pasta Primavera, has just been served. As I'm taking my second bite, who walks in? Demetri, Maggi's father.

Demetri is not happy and, without any greeting, starts yelling at me. "Who the hell are you having my man arrested? Peter Gerhardt is my agent representing Parrhasius Shipping."

Magdalen lays her fork down and stares at her father with a gaze I've never seen before. She slowly rises and lights into him with a verbal assault I never imagined she was capable of.

"You expect George to assign the Boehringer's shipping contract to Parrhasius Shipping so you could siphon off 20 percent of the shipping fees? I told you we are building a respectable company! We are in this for the long haul, not to milk customers for short-term profit!!" That was just her opening barrage. As she thundered her fury grew. I almost felt sorry for Demetri as he was forced out of the restaurant under a flurry of verbal attacks.

Maggi sat back down and took a bite of the Penne Pasta Primavera, "This is really very good," she said in a voice that belied her volcanic verbal attack we had just witnessed.

The next morning I told Maggi I was going out for coffee and a short walk; she should stay in bed and enjoy her temporary freedom from little George, who had a habit of jumping on our bed at daybreak.

My actual destination was Demetri's townhouse, two blocks away. I found him sitting on his patio with a newspaper and a cappuccino. As he got up, he started apologizing, but I waved him down. He asked me to sit and told the maid to bring me a coffee "Or would you prefer a cappuccino?"

As we talked he told me of his ownership of Parrhasius Shipping and again apologized for his presumption of interfering in my business. We spent some time talking about many things before we got to Magdalen. "She is a brilliant woman, I should listen to her," he said, implying I should do the same. "She is like her mother, calm and deliberate, but beware, if her family is threatened, she becomes 'Lyssa,' the Greek goddess of fury."

As I'm getting ready to leave, Demetri tells me with a smile, "Peter is one of those odious people I'm stuck with in my line of work. Your method of sidelining him was brilliant."

***

The next day Magi and I have a two o'clock flight back to Corfu. On our way to the airport, she suggests we stop at her father's nightclub so she could make peace with him. We find Demetri inventorying his bar stock.

"We'll have two 'sidecars,'" I say as we walk in.

He looks up at his daughter, and the two embrace as if nothing happened. His first words are, "I'm selling Parrhasius Shipping. With your new position on the Shipping Guild's board, I could be an embarrassment to you.

"That's a wise move," I say, "but not for that reason. Magi is setting her focus on outing corruption. Shipping companies offering kickbacks and their shipping brokers will be publicized, government audits encouraged, and potential customers warned off. I expect Parrhasius Shipping's stock value will drop over the next twelve months. On the other hand, I expect BSB Co.'s value to soar."

Demetri looks at me and, with a grin, says, "You planned this."

"Let's just say it's a fortunate side effect," I say as I'm helping Magi with her jacket.

31: Dr. Brown

Late in the year, I got an unexpected call from Archie, Dr. Brown. It had been nearly two years since I had worked with the good doctor. He asked if I could meet him in Athens early next week. Never one to turn down an opportunity, I agreed.

The morning I was to meet Archie, I called Nicholas, "What are you doing today? I am meeting an old contact from the University of Manchester at ten. Would you like to join me?"

"Why would I want to do that?" Nicholas asks.

"Well, he usually digs up the good stuff and is not reluctant to let some pieces slip out of the government minder's sight."

Close to the prescribed meeting time, Nicholas and I are sitting in the hotel lobby sipping coffee. Archie walks up and, sitting across from me, asks, "Who is your friend?"

"Archie, meet Nicholas, my cousin. Since you and I last did business, Nicholas and I have entered into a loose confederation, not a partnership, mind you, to work together. His interests are in the Hellenistic period while I am still focused on the older artifacts."

Still somewhat skeptical, Archie suggests we move our meeting down the street to a café. "There are too many ears in this lobby."

A half block down the street we find a café with outside tables that suit Archie's desire for anonymity. He selects a table on the fringe. The waitress comes, we order, coffee is served, and we sit there looking at Archie, waiting for him to speak.

In a conspiratorial tone, he leans in and starts, "I'm heading up a new dig on Cyprus, on the Turkish side of the island. We have a site dating to 3,000 BC, possibly a Minoan settlement, one of the few not on Crete."

"That's fascinating," I say, but how does that involve us? "We're not particularly interested in tempting Turkish authorities, as you said, are watching you like hawks."

Archie pauses, looks at both of us, and in a whisper says, "We've uncovered a large hoard of gold jewelry. If my Turkish minder finds out, he will confiscate it, fund his family's retirement account, and the jewelry never to see the light of day again. We expect Greek overseers to be unethical, but they are people we can work with. But the Turks, they define the term corruption."

"Again, interesting, but where do we come in?"

"I want you to smuggle it to the Greek side of the island. You keep one half, and I get half," Archie says.

Nicholas has been quiet up to this point. "Let us think about your proposal Dr. Brown. Can we get back to you this afternoon?"

"Yes, but please, our time is running out if we're to make this work."

126

32: Uncle Alexander

Back at Vrettos Antiques, Nicholas and I are mulling over Archie's proposal when Elena interrupts, "George, there is a man here asking for you. He scares me."

Nicholas and I set aside our discussion of Brown's proposal and go into the store's sales area where a large elderly man with a sour expression is waiting. He looks familiar.

Without preamble, "Are your George Basdakis? And I assume you are Nicholas. I'm your uncle, Uncle Alexander. Invite me back to your sitting area, and I will tell you our family history."

The three of us go into the back room; Nicholas asks Elena to get some refreshments for our guest.

Uncle Alexander starts with the family history we already know. My father and his younger brother, Mecho, were in the underground fighting Georgios Papadopoulos's dictatorship. "Your father made some serious enemies when he and Mecho firebombed the home of a minor official, killing his elderly parents.

They were forced to leave Greece or face a firing squad. Your father and Mecho both chose to flee, your mother with them. Christos, Nicholas's father, was guilty by association, and he and his wife also left. The families moved to Biloxi, Mississippi," said Alexander.

"I know all that," I said.

"Did your father ever talk about his older brother?" asked Alexander. "We were always at odds, even as children. While he opposed Papadopoulos's dictatorship, I was a member of the regime, working in intelligence collection. Your father put me in a very uncomfortable position, arrest my brothers or join them. I chose the former, but before you judge me, I turned a blind eye when they boarded the cargo ship going to Marseille; escaping my arrest warrants.

Since then, I've risen to the head of state security. It seems I hold too many secrets to be terminated, so I'm a perpetual member of the government, regardless of which party is in charge."

So they escaped because you let them? said Nicolas.

"Yes. Since then I've watched from afar, contacting Christos every few years. I know of his smuggling operation. And I've watched you George, and your company, Basdakis Shipping Brokerage. You Nicholas slipped under my radar until recently. Your father still thinks you died in Iraq."

"Not to be rude," says Uncle Alexander, "I need to talk with George privately. Let me suggest you and I adjourn to the café on the corner."

As we were seating ourselves, Alexander said, "I was impressed with your people moving operation in Brazil. Dillion gave me all the details."

129

"Dillion? What does the FBI have to do with this," I ask, now somewhat worried.

"Don't worry about the FBI. That case is closed as far as they are concerned. But just for your information, Dillion said he was most impressed with your ingenuity."

"Now, I didn't seek you out to talk about the past. I'm here to see if you would be interested in working for me."

"I know about Dr. Brown's offer … we want to encourage you to take it. We have an undercover agent on his team and need someone, you, to retrieve the information he has collected on Turkish military installations. If you accept his offer, I'll provide you cover, and here is the best part, you and Nicolas can keep whatever Brown gives you."

"I have to think about it," I say.

"No, it's decision time now. You owe Dr. Brown a call, and I need a little time to put my assets in place."

After a quick assessment of my uncle's offer, I say, "Let's keep it in the family; I'm in."

33: Escape

It wasn't hard to get Nicholas's buy-in. The prospect of easy money was too hard for him to resist.

It was much harder convincing Maggi. I was forced to tell her the whole story, and of Alexander's intent to enlist me in the country's intelligence service. Learning this enterprise had the State's support, she relented but was still skeptical.

Two days later, Nicholas and I touched down at the International Airport in Larnaca, Cyprus.

Archie meets us with his Land Rover. "I think we should go straight to the dig," says Archie. It's about twenty kilometers north of the Greek/Turkish debarkation line, an hour's drive from here.

Thomas is now Archie's deputy and is in charge of the dig's day-to-day operations. He gives us a tour of the site, pointing out the Turkish minder with his military contingent. He finishes the tour, taking us to a nearby guesthouse where Archie has reserved two rooms for us.

We find Archie at the bar. "You didn't mention your minder has military support," I snap at him. Both Nicolas and I are pissed at Archie for this. Perhaps, more accurately, his deception to tell us about the Turkish military. Abandoning the project and returning to Larnaca in the morning is becoming a viable option.

"We'll pick this up in the morning," I say as Nicholas and I walk out.

Leaving the bar, Nicolas heads to the guesthouse. I tell him I'll be there in a bit; I need to talk to Thomas to get a little more information.

I head over to the tents housing the archaeological team. "Where can I find Thomas?" I ask one of the young college students.

Thomas is in the last tent, set off by itself. Entering his tent unannounced, I say, "Czar Alexi sent me."

Thomas looks up with a surprised expression, "Since when have you been working for the government?"

"About four days now," I say. "Our handler tells me you have documents that need to go to him."

Thomas looks around and pulls out a small pack of papers folded into a neat square in a Ziplock bag. "Don't let these out of your sight, or we're both screwed!"

In our room, Nicholas and I continue to review our options. "I don't like this," Nicholas says, "If the Turks get wind of this, we could be dead or, at best, serving a twenty-year sentence in a Turkish jail for smuggling artifacts."

"I agree. Let's head home in the morning."

We're up at first light, skipping breakfast. We load our gear into the Land Rover and are a couple of miles up the road when my phone beeps. I look at it, it's Archie. I'm inclined not to answer, but on second thought, I take his call and put it on speaker.

"George, I'm disappointed you left without saying goodbye."

"And the point of your call is?" I ask.

"Well, George, I consider our deal still in force. Last night, thinking you might bolt this morning, I put the jewelry in the vehicle, inside the backseat cushions. That was our planned extraction method all along. We had duplicate seats stored off-site and transferred the horde over the last few days into them. Last night we swapped the seats with those in your vehicle. I'll meet you at the dock tomorrow."

"You bastard!"

"Come, come, George, you two are going to make a small fortune on this. You'll thank me." And with that, he disconnected.

I'm driving, gripping the wheel in sheer anger. "He's your friend," grunts Nicholas, "but I'm going to kill him."

"No, he's mine."

We have passed the Turkish checkpoint and are getting close to the Greek side when I see a police vehicle's flashing lights cresting the hill behind us. It's closing fast. I tell Nicholas to hold on as I press the accelerator to the floor. The Land Rover leaps forward, a quarter mile to the demarcation line. Someone in the police vehicle is firing an automatic rifle. The back window is blown out, and the rear left tire is hit. I'm knocked forward into the steering wheel.

The Greek guards are now returning fire with a heavy machine gun. The police vehicle erupts into a fireball. I lose control, the Land Rover careens into the ditch next to the road. It flips two, maybe three times before I pass out.

I'm drifting in and out of consciousness. I see the ambulance's blue lights, faces of the rescue team, and in my peripheral vision, there's Fat Leonard whispering… *"Always Check for Junk."*

End (maybe)

Also by Don Allen

Satisfaction

Upon retirement from the Army's Rangers, Sean Murphy goes to work for his former Commanding Officer, Colonel Anderson - a man with many contacts. The company's name is Eyeball Inc. It specializes in providing unspecified services to the Nation's alphabet agencies. Sean soon finds he was safer tracking bad guys in Afghanistan. His first assignment goes sideways. North Koreans are after him, the FBI wants him, and drug dealers fear him. His adventures take him to Lakeview, Oregon, where he poses as a doctor prior to becoming the town's deputy sheriff, to Long Island, where he rescues his two grandchildren kidnapped by agents of the North Korean UN delegation, and finally, the capture of a cartel drug lord in Texas's Big Bend country. In the end, he gets satisfaction in Istanbul.

Dog Walker

Another fast-paced 'dime novel' that can be read in one afternoon on the beach or sitting in an airline coach's center seat. Our hero, Samuel Goodwin, and his dog Maxie, recently retired from the Boston Police Department's Canine Division, become entangled in Islamic terrorist plots. Sam's neighbor, a Yazidi refugee, is targeted by the former manager of the Mosel Rape Hotel, whom she recently recognized in downtown Boston. Two recently retired BPD detectives nicknamed Salt 'n Pepper, go into the PI business. Their first case, locating missing waitstaff from Boston's Chinatown restaurants, leads them to The Islamic Society of Boston. The Islamic Society has concocted a plan to poison New York City's water supply. Two ISIS terrorists sneak across the southern border, with cartel help, to become the Society's foot soldiers. The above cast of characters comes together to create a fascinating story.

If you enjoyed this story or have
comments, please let me know at:
dons-home@cox.net

Should there be a George Basdakis sequel?

www.ingramcontent.com/pod-product-compliance
Lightning Source LLC
Chambersburg PA
CBHW071309130626
46556CB00004B/1537